The Songwriter's Rival
Sweet Country Music Romance: Book 3
Penelope Spark

I0620714

Chapter 1

Hannah grudgingly closed her office window. The neighbors were at it again, and Hannah couldn't handle the distraction. Even though she believed the fresh air helped her creativity, she would have to live without it for now. Besides, her boss, the great Suzette Walker, always harped on her for letting all the hard-fought A/C fly out the window into the Nashville humidity. When Hannah had first started working at Platinum Publishing, they hadn't even *had* air conditioning, which was ridiculous. She used to play her keyboard with fans blowing at her from four different directions and her sheet music taped to the music rack. Hannah had been hassling Suzette, whom some, particularly Logan Hawkins, called Suzie Q, to move to Music Row, where all the action was. Instead, Suzette had installed air conditioners. Suzette had called it a compromise.

Platinum Publishing was located in East Nashville, which Hannah thought was weird. But when Suzette had bootstrapped her beginnings, the fixer-upper in the residential neighborhood was what she could afford. And when Suzette had hired Hannah, she was too grateful to complain. Now that Hannah had made a name for herself in the songwriting community, she *could* throw her weight around and demand that Suzette move to a more traditional address, but Hannah would never do that. She had no intention of ever gettin' above her raisin'.

And so, there she was, alone in the old house well after dark, trying to fix a broken song's stubborn bridge, while her hippie neighbors partied. Hannah had nothing against hippies in general; she just didn't love her neighbors. Platinum Publishing sat directly beside The Purple

Oasis, a communal living complex full of perpetually happy, perpetually loud people.

She sat down in front of her keyboard and let her fingers hover over the keys, hoping something would happen.

Nothing did.

She allowed her fingers to fall onto random keys, which made a terrible sound that was satisfyingly discordant. She was about to hang her head when her peripheral vision caught some movement near the open doorway. She almost didn't want to look. She was alone in this old house, late at night. Nothing should be moving in her doorway.

She took a deep breath and then slowly turned her head. At first, she saw nothing. Then, near the floor, almost lying on the threshold, she saw a white oval shape. The soft light in her office forced her to squint to see that it was in fact a hockey mask with two eyes peering out at her through it. Under normal circumstances, this would have scared the tar out of her, but she'd been working with Logan Hawkins for over a year, and she immediately recognized this terrible sight for what it was: Logan's idea of humor.

He was so obnoxious.

Without taking her eyes off the mask, she reached for something to throw at him. The first thing her fingers touched was a stapler, and her fingers hungrily curled around its heft. This could actually hurt him. Trying not to telegraph her play, she wound the stapler at his head.

Of course, he jerked out of the way in time. She'd never been much of an athlete.

"Jerk!" she hollered out into the hallway, which now looked empty, but she knew it wasn't. She heard him scramble to his feet and then one hand appeared in her doorway, waving.

"Okay, okay! I surrender! Don't throw any more office utensils at me!" He stepped into view, the creepy plastic mask now in his hand, and flashed her an enormous smile. "There was a day that this mask would've had you screaming bloody murder."

"There was a day when you hadn't worn me down."

He laughed and collapsed onto her worn leather couch.

"I didn't invite you to sit down."

He made no move to get up.

"Seriously, I have work to do. What are you doing here so late, anyway?" Logan *never* worked late.

"I could ask you the same thing."

This made no sense. Hannah *always* worked late. Hard work meant success, and it wasn't like she had a social life to run off to. But she supposed there was a chance Logan hadn't noticed her extended work hours. He never noticed anything that didn't directly affect him. Logan cared about one thing: Logan.

"I'm working," she said through clenched teeth.

He still didn't move.

"I'm serious, Logan. Get out of my office." She stood and moved toward the door, hoping that would spur him into action.

Instead, he tipped over and rested his head on the arm of her couch. "Go ahead. Work. I'm just going to take a little snooze."

She was not amused. "Logan!" she hollered. She stormed toward him and then kicked her own couch. This did nothing. She reached down and shook his arm. "I'm serious! Get out!" She would have to talk to Suzette about him again, though she didn't know what good it would do. Logan made Suzette a lot of money. She wasn't about to fire him just because Hannah couldn't stand him.

"I'm serious too," he said, sleepiness slurring his words. "I need to sleep, and I don't want to go home. Otis has to spend the night at the vet's, and my apartment is too quiet without him."

Right. She'd forgotten. Logan cared about *two* things: himself and his *dog*.

"Go ahead and work," he said, his eyes still closed. "Sing me to sleep."

He really wasn't going to move. She stood there glaring down at him, her fists clenched at her side. She hated him. What a presumptuous little twit! She couldn't work with him lying there! As much as she couldn't stand him, he was a talented songwriter himself, and she wasn't about to troubleshoot her stubborn bridge within his earshot so that he could lie there silently critiquing every note. And he might not even do it silently.

But what could she do? She didn't want to be the whiny little tattletale who called her boss in the middle of the night. So, she gave up. She turned off her desktop, her keyboard, and her light, and walked out of her office. She didn't want to go home yet, but she'd rather hang out in her apartment than try to get anything done with Logan on her couch.

Of course, he'd left the front door unlocked. As Hannah turned around to lock it, a lilting voice asked, "Where did the cowboy go?"

Hannah turned toward The Purple Oasis. A pretty woman with long, blond dreadlocks sat illuminated by the porch light.

"He's not a cowboy."

"Whatever." The woman giggled. "But did he go in there? He said he had to go to bed, but his truck's still here." She pointed her chin at his truck, and Hannah realized that he was blocking her car in. She groaned.

Parking was a perpetual problem at Platinum. Their building had originally been a house—with a narrow driveway that would be appropriate for a house. This problem was easily solved by parking on the street, which all of them usually did. When Hannah had come back from getting some dinner, everyone else had gone home, so she'd simply pulled into the driveway. Then, apparently, Logan had acted like he owned the place, and had parked immediately behind her.

Hannah looked at the woman. "He was with you guys tonight?" For some reason, this idea bothered her.

She nodded and stood up. Her long flowing dress swayed around her slender legs. "So, is he in there?"

Hannah nodded. "Yep." Then she unlocked the door and went back inside.

Of course, she found him right where she'd left him. She flipped the light on and grabbed his upper arm. She shook him again—hard this time. His upper body rocked back and forth, and his head flopped around so dramatically that she suspected he was doing it on purpose, but he didn't acknowledge her. She shook him again. "Are you drunk?"

One eye popped open. "Of course not. I don't drink. You know that."

She knew no such thing. She knew he *said* he didn't drink, but she didn't believe anything that came off this man's charming silver tongue. "Then why are you so tired?"

"Because it's the middle of the night. Why *aren't* you tired?" Half his mouth grinned. "And why are you still holding onto my arm?"

She yanked her hand away. "I'm not."

He made a big show of rolling over. "Do you have any blankets?"

Of course she had blankets. She often slept on this couch herself. But she wasn't going to cover him up with her own blankets on her own couch like some attentive nanny. "I do not."

"Yes you do. Top of your cabinet."

That was it. The anger that had been building up within her burst out through her normally polite mouth. "Logan Hawkins!" she screamed, and he started. "Get off my couch!" She held her arm out straight, her index finger pointing to her door.

He turned his head toward her, his eyes wide. Then he sat up. "Seriously?" All the playfulness had left his voice. "I was just messing around. No need to get all shook up."

She *was* shook up, literally shaking in fact, and he telling her *not* to be shook up just made it worse. She stepped closer to him and lowered her voice. "Are you kidding me? You come into *my* office and interrupt *my* work and now *you're* the one who gets to be offended? I don't think so!"

He smirked. "Fine." He smashed the ball of his hand into one of his eye sockets and rubbed vigorously. "I'll go sleep in my office. I was just trying to be neighborly." He stepped toward the door and she quickly moved to block him.

"No, first you go move your truck."

He chuckled. "Oh yeah, that's right. Sorry. When I parked there, I didn't plan to stay long." He reached into his pocket and pulled out his keys. "But now that I'm getting into the truck, I might as well just go home. I'm wide awake now, anyway," he said, as if that was all her fault.

Chapter 2

Logan paused before walking into work and stared at The Purple Oasis. As ridiculous as the name of her community home was, Willow had been sweet and cute, and he'd enjoyed getting to know her the night before. But this morning, the large house was quiet and still, its residents either at work already or still sleeping. It was probably for the best. He'd liked spending time with her, but he didn't want her to think he was falling in love or anything. He laughed at the thought as he walked inside.

"You're late," Suzie Q called from inside her office.

"Just barely." He wasn't worried. She always liked to hassle him, but he knew she'd never get rid of him. He stuck his head into her office as he passed and flashed her the same smile he'd been flashing women since he'd figured out how well it worked on his mother. "I promise, I'll make it up to you. Any news?"

She didn't look impressed. "If there were news, I would've texted you. Get to work."

He held up both hands and wiggled them. "Now, now. Can't rush genius. Got to wait for inspiration to strike." This was not true for him, but pretending to believe it better allowed him to follow his own schedule—or lack thereof. He flashed her another smile and then headed down the hallway toward his office, which was so small he often wondered what poor child had grown up in a bedroom so tiny.

It was still obvious that the building had once been a family's home. The living room, which was out front, was still very much a living room. People hung out in there when they felt the need for social stimulation, and that was where the writers played their songs for artists. A lot of dreams had been realized in that room. Even more had been smashed to pieces. Most of Logan's had been realized, and though he acted cocky, he was truly grateful for all the success he'd had. He knew he'd been lucky.

Suzie Q had turned the dining room into a conference room that also served as her office. The kitchen was still the kitchen, and it was his favorite room.

Each of the songwriter's got a bedroom, transformed into a creative office—although, Hannah often slept in hers, so it was still sort of a bedroom. He'd *tried* to sleep in there last night, but she'd had some sort of fit. He still couldn't believe how upset she'd been. Sure, he understood how annoying it was to be interrupted while working, but she didn't usually get *that* mad. He paused in front of her door, which was cracked open, and rapped on it with his knuckles.

She didn't answer. He nudged the door open and saw that she wasn't at her desk or her keyboard. He pushed the door open further to check the couch, but nada.

"Can I help you?" she snapped from the hallway behind him.

He jumped but then turned and gave her his best smile. "I just wanted to say good morning, and to apologize for last night." He eyed the jelly donut in her hand. It looked like raspberry—his favorite.

She raised an eyebrow, and it was cute. He'd always thought that she was pretty, with her round face and high cheekbones. She had huge brown eyes that sparkled when she sang. Her thick dark hair would probably be gorgeous if she wore it down, but she never did. It was always coiled into a perfectly symmetrical, painfully tight bun on the back of her head. He imagined that this hairstyle saved her time. Hannah Carter didn't have room in her schedule for such vanities as primping. She was in too much of a hurry. In a hurry for what, he had no idea. But she was always in a hurry. Everything was always life or death. This girl had no idea how to relax. "And just what are you sorry for, exactly?"

He had no idea. He put the smile back on his face, hoping this would be enough.

It wasn't.

"I'm sorry for interrupting your work last night."

She hesitated, then gave him a dirty look and brushed by him into her office, taking her beautiful jelly donut with her. He turned to ask her to split it with him, but she slammed the door in his face. He put his hands on his hips and sighed. He'd tried and tried to be friends with this woman, and she just wasn't having it. Maybe he should stop trying. When they'd met, he'd felt sorry for her. She was always so stressed out. He'd tried to loosen her up with some fun, get her laughing, but it hadn't worked. She was still the same stick-in-the-mud she'd been when they'd met, and he was tired of her crankiness.

There in that hallway, staring at her closed door, he silently vowed to stop trying. Stop trying to be her friend. Stop trying to make her laugh. Feeling good about his vow, he headed for the kitchen.

He hadn't taken two steps when he realized that he really shouldn't vow to stop messing with her altogether. It was too much fun. He would stop trying to make *her* laugh, but he might still pull the occasional prank to make *himself* laugh. She was, after all, his favorite person to prank. Sure, the hockey mask hadn't done much damage last night, but usually, his antics really freaked her out, and this brought extra splashes of fun into his life.

The box of donuts sat open on the counter. Chloe held what looked like a chocolate glazed up to her mouth. "Good morning, sunshine!" Chloe was his friend. She liked his pranks. She liked *him*. And he liked her back. She and he had written a couple of really good songs together. He looked into the box: one plain old-fashioned donut sat alone in the middle of the box, surrounded by tiny piles of powdered sugar, a few sprinkles, and several jelly smears. He looked up at Chloe. "Why does Alex buy old-fashioned? No one likes old-fashioned donuts!" He was genuinely sad, but she laughed at him sans sympathy.

"Alex likes old-fashioned," she said through a full mouth.

He didn't know if this was true, but he decided to teach the office manager a lesson by eating her allegedly favorite flavor of donut. He picked up the old-fashioned and headed for the coffee pot.

Chapter 3

Hannah finally finished the song she'd been working on the night before, before Logan had tried to force her into a slumber party. She picked up the sheet music, and a tremendous sense of accomplishment washed over her. This one could be big. She rolled her head, trying to get the kinks out of her neck, and then headed for Suzette's office.

She met Logan in the narrow hallway and pushed her hip toward the wall to get out of his way.

"Your neck okay?" He actually managed to sound concerned. She knew that he wasn't, but he sounded it.

She dropped her hand from her neck. "I'm fine."

"You sure?" He held up his hands and wiggled his fingers. "I am a miracle masseuse!" He said this in a weird voice, as though he was trying to imitate an accent, but if that was an actual accent, she had no idea what region of the world it belonged to.

For just a second, she was tempted, imagining how good his large, probably strong hands with their calloused guitar-string-fingers would feel against her tight, sore muscles, but she pushed that idea out of her mind as fast as she could. "Really? So you could smear poison ivy all over your hands before you did it?" She passed him and kept walking.

He snorted. "What? That doesn't even make sense. Then I'd have poison ivy too!"

She didn't turn around, pretending she hadn't heard him. He was right. What she'd said hadn't made sense, but he'd offered to rub her neck, and whenever Logan offered anything, there was always a catch. There was always a prank, a trick, a shock, a something. So she'd just live with a stiff neck. It wasn't a new problem to her. Long hours at the keyboard often led to her slouching, and though she made a conscious effort to sit up straight, she didn't always succeed.

She knocked on Suzette's door and stepped partly inside. "I finished! And I think you're going to like this one."

Suzette looked up, looking stressed. She held out a hand for the music. "Good, because I need your help with something. Can you go get Logan for me? I need to talk to you two."

You can't be serious.

Suzette read her body language. "I know, I know, you two have this rivalry thing going, but I need you to be professionals for a second."

"It's not a rivalry," Hannah said, beyond annoyed. Suzette was making her sound like a teenage cheerleader. "He is obnoxious and distracting and refuses to take anything serious—"

"Just go get him," Suzette almost snapped.

Instantly remorseful that she'd frustrated Suzette, Hannah turned to do as she'd been asked.

"And Hannah?"

Hannah turned back. "Yes?"

Suzette smiled, and her lilac lipstick reflected some of the light from her desk lamp. "I always like your stuff."

"Thanks, Boss." A little comforted, Hannah headed down the hall toward Logan's office.

She could hear him picking before she got there. Huh, the guy was actually working. She hated to interrupt. Truth be told, Hannah was a little jealous of Logan's success. Not of his *songs*—she thought those were utter rubbish—but of his success. They were both hot new names on the songwriting front, but his songs just seemed to fall out of the sky and into his lap. She'd never seen him struggle for anything.

He looked up before she could knock. "Finally! You've come to visit." Unusually, he *didn't* smile. Logan always smiled.

"Not exactly." She looked around his office and saw why he'd tried to crash on *her* couch. His was buried in stuff. In fact, the whole office was. How could he stand to work like this? She found even the suggestion of clutter to be a distraction. "Suzette wants to talk to us." She turned to go.

"Both of us?"

"That's what she said," Hannah said, facing away from him. She waved for him to follow her.

"At the same time?"

Was he daft? She stopped and turned. "I would imagine so."

He still hadn't gotten out of his chair.

"Hurry up." She didn't wait for him. She went back the way she'd come, eager to show Suzette that she was the more dutiful one, even though everyone in the building knew that. Probably everyone in Nashville knew that.

She sat down and smiled at Suzette, and then they waited for Mr. Punctual.

When he finally arrived, Suzette told him to shut the door behind him. This was odd. What was going on?

Logan sat down and flashed his pearly whites at Suzette. "Why, Suzie Q! Have you done something new with your hair?"

Hannah rolled her eyes as Suzette ran a hand over the side of her head, which smoothed out the poof for a fraction of a second. As soon as she removed her hand, the hair bounced back into place. No, she hadn't done anything differently. It looked exactly like it always looked, and Logan was *such* a kiss-up.

Suzette leaned back in her chair and folded her hands across her abdomen. She surveyed them carefully. Everything about this scene was so unusual that Hannah's stomach was doing flips. Suzette's eyes landed on Logan. "I have some good news."

Logan ran his hands down his quads as if he was smoothing out his jeans—which were tight and plenty smooth already. "All right. I love good news."

"Your song, 'Can't Lose You' —"

"Yeah?" He leaned toward her, his impatience palpable.

"Cole Washburne might want to cut it."

Hannah expected him to smile, but he didn't. "*Might* want to? What does that mean?" He scowled. Hannah had never seen him so serious.

Suzette shifted her gaze to Hannah. "This is where you come in."

Oh no. This didn't sound good. "I'm sorry?"

Suzette took a long breath. "He really wants to cut it, but he says the chorus isn't quite right yet—"

"Seriously?" Logan said, his voice an octave lower than usual.

Suzette narrowed her eyes. "You can say no. You can tell him you won't change the song. But if Cole Washburne cuts it, and if he releases it as a single, you know what that could mean."

Hannah still didn't follow. Was *she* supposed to fix the chorus?

They sat there silently for a minute that felt much longer.

Finally, Suzette said, "I want you two to work together. Cole thinks the song is too easy. He used the word *flippant*. He wants a deeper chorus. I know that Hannah can do that for you."

Logan turned his head and looked at Hannah. He managed to look offended, as if she'd dreamed up this game plan. "Well, I'm sure she can do that for me, but I can also just do it all by myself."

"No. This will be faster. We don't want him to forget about the song and cut something else. I want you to start right now. Hannah just finished a song. You put down the song you're working on, and revise this one. Between the two of you, it shouldn't take any time at all."

This was the first time Hannah had ever disagreed with Suzette. Hannah knew about creative synergy, when you get two creative forces together and the outcome is greater than a sum of the separate parts. She'd even experienced it before. But not with the likes of Logan Hawkins.

"Go get started, please." Suzette wasn't kidding around.

By the time Hannah had pushed herself out of her chair, Logan had already left the room.

"Thank you for this," Suzette said softly. "This could be huge for Platinum."

Hannah didn't know if she meant huge for Platinum's bank account or reputation or both, but Hannah would do it for Suzette. "I'll do the best I can."

"You always do, and I appreciate it."

Chapter 4

"Wait!" Hannah called after Logan. "Let's work in my office. There's more room!"

"I'm just going to get my guitar!" he hollered back without turning around. He was well aware that there was more room in her office. Did she think he was going to write without his guitar? He stopped in the middle of his office and tried to calm down. He was so angry, and he was embarrassed at how angry he was. This wasn't a big deal. Songwriters got revision requests all the time. Why hadn't Washburne just rewritten the chorus himself? He'd probably tried and failed, and that's how it had ended up back in Logan's lap. But why had Suzie Q assigned him a helper? Like he was in junior high and needed a tutor. He could have fixed that chorus himself. He wasn't a simpleton. He could have filled that chorus with so much poetic bologna that Washburne would have had the ladies swooning. He grabbed his guitar. Enough chewing his cud. *Let's get this over with.*

He forced a smile back onto his lips before entering Hannah's office. She'd moved a chair closer to her keyboard and now she patted it. "Make yourself comfortable."

He sat, but he was far from comfortable.

She turned toward her keys, but didn't reach for them. "For what it's worth, I'm sorry about this. I know you must be pretty irritated."

"I'm fine." He chuckled. "Really. Fine as a twine mine." He looked into her eyes. "So, let's get started."

She nodded. "I'm afraid I don't know the song well. Can you sing it for me?"

He wasn't in the mood, but he obliged, delivering the song without any heart at all. He'd written it months ago, and he hadn't really liked it then. Now, it made him feel ill. He wrapped it up without flourish.

"That's a very sweet song."

He let his elbow hang over his guitar and scratched at his stubble. Her gaze was making him self-conscious. "Thanks."

"No." She laughed, and he didn't know why. "I mean it. It's *really* sweet. I can see why Cole wants to cut it. And frankly ..." Her voice trailed off.

"Frankly, what?"

She shrugged. "I'm not sure. I guess I've just always been impressed by your love songs."

Was she trying to make him feel better? Because if so, it wasn't working.

"Really. They're so heartfelt, so ... well, *serious*." She leaned toward him and rested her forearms on her legs. A few stray curls had escaped her bun and now fell into her eyes. She blew them away and he realized he was paying too much attention to her hair. "I mean, I think I know you a little, and you just don't seem like the type of man who would actually say these things to a woman."

He barked out a laugh. "Of course not!"

She leaned back abruptly.

Still laughing, he explained, "If I wrote things I really mean, I'd be writing about jelly donuts. I don't write what I think. I write what will *sell*. And so, with love songs, I ask myself, 'Self, what is a woman dying to hear her man say?' and then I just say it on a record that she can buy." He paused, but he couldn't read the expression on Hannah's face. This made him nervous so he kept talking. "I don't think *any* man would say the words of this song to a woman. And it won't be men who buy this record from Washburne."

She held up one hand. "Okay, I think I've heard enough." Her voice was toneless. A poker voice.

What had he said wrong? Had he shattered some idea she'd had about love songs? Surely not. Surely she had known that songwriters write things simply to sell them, not to bare their souls. If not, she was more naive than he'd thought. A question popped into his mind. Had he ever heard a love song come out of Hannah? He didn't think so. How had she sold so many songs already without any love songs? "Do you even write love songs?"

She flinched. "Not really."

He could tell she didn't want him to ask the question. He asked it anyway. "Why not?"

She shrugged. "I try to dig a little deeper." She looked at the keyboard. "Give me the chorus again."

He gave it to her.

She closed her eyes and listened, and for reasons he didn't understand, he worked harder this time to make the chorus sound better, to make her like it.

When he finished, her eyes popped open. "Yeah, I can see why Cole wants something different."

"Oh yeah? Why?"

"Because it's cheesy."

He snorted. "This is country. Cheesy works."

She shook her head slowly. "It's too cheesy. And Cole doesn't usually record cheesy stuff." She took a deep breath. "We might have to change the title."

He shrugged one shoulder and sank back into the couch. "Do what you gotta do. Let's get this over with."

Chapter 5

Hannah felt bad for Logan. He seemed to be taking this hard. She wished Suzette hadn't picked her. She knew that if Suzette had picked an older, more experienced writer to help Logan, he wouldn't be so irritated. But Logan was right: the faster they got this done, the faster they could move on with their lives.

She took a deep breath. She needed to tactfully tell him that the chorus was terrible. "Well, I think the whole point of the song is that the narrator can't live without this woman, right?"

He did nothing to respond.

"So, if he's claiming that this loss is going to kill him, I think we need a more sober feel to the chorus—"

"Just do it, Hannah."

"I don't want to *just do it*," she snapped. Instantly, she felt bad for her tone. This was one of her peers here, a fellow artist—even if he didn't always act like an artist, he was one, and she wanted to be sensitive to that. She took a breath. "I'm trying to be respectful of your piece here. I don't want to just rip it to shreds. I want to honor it and you, so I need you to participate in this process."

He didn't look convinced.

"Or we might lose what verve this song already has," she added.

He smiled, and it looked genuine, not like his usual smarmy grin. "Verve. I like that word." He looked down at his guitar and strummed. "I think I'm going to use that in a song."

Good. He was happy again. "Excellent, but let's focus on this song for now. I don't think verve quite fits here."

He waggled his eyebrows at her. "It could."

She smiled, despite herself, and shook her head. "First, I think we need to do away with the na-na-na."

He nodded without hesitation. "Yeah, those na's were only there because I didn't have lyrics to fit that melody."

She succeeded in not rolling her eyes. It really annoyed her when songwriters did the na-na thing. And yet, almost without fail, when they did do it, listeners loved it. Apparently, people loved to sing along with repetitive nonsensical syllables. "And why do you talk about booze in your songs if you're not a drinker?"

He shrugged. "Booze sells. And I don't care if other people drink. It's just not my shtick."

She laughed at his use of the word *shtick* and then stopped herself. Why was she laughing at him? It only encouraged him. She reminded herself that she needed to get this done as fast as possible, so she could get back to her own songs. "Okay, well, I think that with this song, the booze isn't helping."

"But it rhymes with lose!" he whined.

She didn't know if he was kidding. She hoped so. "So do lots of other words. In fact, I was thinking about adding a setting to the song, as a way to ground it."

"Ground it?" His voice was edged with criticism. "Did it not get home before curfew?"

Again, she didn't know if he was serious. "No, I mean grounding as in bringing it down to earth, making it relatable."

His face was blank.

"Do you remember where you were when you wrote this song?"

He strummed again. "In my office."

That wasn't helpful. "Okay, well, where else could someone be while they were thinking about not losing someone?"

He tipped his head and narrowed his eyes. "This is stupid."

"Just think. Where would you go if you were sad?"

Something flickered across his face and his eyes dropped. If she didn't know better, she'd think he had just felt emotional pain. Was that even possible for Logan? She wanted to ask, to push, because that would probably really help the song, but she didn't quite dare.

"I would go to a rodeo." He sang the word rodeo and then shook his head. "Nope, doesn't rhyme with lose."

She sighed. "Can you be serious for a single second?"

He let his hand fall onto the guitar as if it were a drum. "I don't know, Hannah. You're acting like a shrink with all these questions. I don't know where I'd go. I'm never sad."

But hadn't that been sadness she'd just seen in his eyes a few seconds ago? "No one is never sad, Logan. Fine. Then just think of a place that someone else might go. One of those people who is going to buy Cole's album."

"Church!" he said quickly. He hit his guitar again. "But that doesn't rhyme with *lose*."

"No, but church *pews* does."

His face lit up. "Yes!" He strummed and sang, "Can't lose you, sittin' in a church pew ..."

That's going to need some work, she thought, but didn't want to discourage him.

He kept singing, "Sittin' in a church pew, praying to re-woo you ..."

She gasped and he stopped, looking at her expectantly. "What?"

"I like it!" Too late, she realized her voice betrayed her surprise.

"Yeah?" He didn't seem offended.

"Yeah, that's good." She hit a chord on her keyboard and resang the lines he'd just created. Then she added, "What am I going to do, can't live without you, can't lose you." She stopped and looked at him. "Just an idea. We can do better."

He began to pick and sing, "Sittin' in this church pew ... don't know how to be me without you ..." He stopped and said, "No, wait," and then sang, "Can't be me without you ... so I'm sittin' in a church pew, prayin' to re-woo you ... begging God—" His voice built into a crescendo on the word God and then he delivered the title with a timing that sent chills racing up her spine—"can't lose you."

"Yes!" she cried, clapping her hands.

He pointed to her music rack. "Write that down, would ya'?"

She laughed again, and realized she was having real fun. When was the last time she'd had fun? She couldn't remember. Maybe writing with Logan wasn't such a bad thing. Maybe they should do it more often. Or maybe this was just a fluke.

"What?" he asked.

"What?" she said back.

"You're staring at me."

"Oh, sorry." She yanked her eyes away. "I was just thinking about the song."

"Sure, sure, all the ladies love to look."

And just like that, she hated him again.

Chapter 6

Logan leaned on Hannah's door frame and folded his arms across his chest, not even trying to hide the pride he was feeling. He opened his mouth to share the good news, but he was interrupted by a piercing scream from the ladies' room.

To her credit, Hannah didn't even flinch. Or maybe this was to his credit. When Hannah had first shown up at Platinum, she'd been jumpy as a wild rabbit, but now, not much seemed to faze her.

She quirked an eyebrow at him. "Is someone trying to murder a junior high cheerleader in our bathroom, or did you do something?"

Out of the corner of his eye, he saw Chloe storming down the hallway, her eyes fixed on him with a glare that could've melted glass. Should he risk Hannah's wrath by ducking into her office uninvited in order to avoid Chloe's fury? Or should he just run for the front door? His indecision paralyzed him and so he was still standing there when Chloe punched him in the shoulder—hard.

"Ow!" he cried, standing up straight so that he could use his good arm to massage his now wounded shoulder. "That hurt!"

"Good!" She still looked mad, and he worried she was going to hit him again. "That wasn't funny, Logan! That really scared me!"

"Aw, come on, it was a little funny. And I'm sorry, it was meant for Hannah."

"What was meant for me?"

He wanted to answer her, but Chloe didn't let him. "And why were you hanging out in the women's bathroom, anyway?"

He leaned on the door frame again and slid his hands into his pockets. He was pretty sure that Chloe was done assaulting him. "I wasn't *hanging* out in there. I made sure no one was in there, and then

I snuck in this morning and did you ladies a favor by replenishing your bathroom tissue supply."

"Sneaked," Hannah said.

"What?" Logan and Chloe asked in unison.

"It's sneaked. Not snuck."

"Oh, whatever." Chloe dismissed the grammar sheriff and turned her glare back on him. "Just know that, when you least expect it, I *will* get my revenge." Then she whirled around and stomped away.

"What did you do to the toilet paper?" Hannah asked.

He shrugged his sore shoulder and gave her a playful look. "If I tell you, then I can't later use the same gag on you."

She shook her head. "Oh please don't. Just tell me what you did."

"Nope." The more she wanted to know, the more he didn't want to tell her.

"Fine! Then what are you doing here?"

"Huh? I work here."

"No, Logan. Why are you hovering in my doorway like some creepy stalker? You looked like you were going to tell me something, but then Chloe found the fake spider in the bathroom and interrupted you."

How had she guessed that? "It wasn't a fake spider. I *drew* a spider on the toilet paper and then rolled it back up—"

"Oh my word." She sounded appalled. "Thank *God* I wasn't the one to find it."

"I did it for you," he said, managing to sound sweet.

"I'm sure you did. Now, you've got ten seconds to tell me your news or I'm reporting you for loitering." She stood up as if she had somewhere to go.

"I just wanted to tell you that Washburne likes the new chorus. He's going to cut the song."

Her eyes sparkled. "Awesome! I knew he'd like it!" She stepped toward him, and for a second, he thought she was going to come hug him, but then she stopped moving and just stood there awkwardly. *Had* she been going to hug him? It wouldn't have been that weird to give him a congratulatory embrace. But now she just stood there staring at him, a little off balance, as if she was in a play and she'd forgotten her line. He didn't know what to say.

"Um ... excuse me?" She pointed at the narrow gap in the doorway that he wasn't taking up. "I need to get through there."

"Oh." He quickly swung himself out of the way, feeling oddly embarrassed. What was happening here? Why were his cheeks hot?

She stopped in the doorway so that they faced each other in the opening that now felt too narrow to be a doorway. She was so close that he could smell her, and she smelled delightful—fresh ... and comfortable. Like fabric softener. She smiled up at him. "And really, congratulations. I'm very, very happy for you." She stood there waiting for him to respond, but he was tongue-tied. He couldn't remember the last time he'd been tongue-tied. She finally gave up waiting and walked away down the hall.

"Happy for both of us," he called after her. Her name was on the song too now. For better or for worse, they were tied together for infinity, and this idea made his chest warm.

Wait. What was going on? Why was he getting all warm and fuzzy about icy Hannah Carter? He shook his head. All this worrying about Otis was turning him into an emotional cuckoo. He had to get some sleep.

Chapter 7

Hannah leaned on the sink, staring at her reflection in the bathroom mirror. She hadn't even had to go to the bathroom, but she'd been such an awkward mess in her office that she needed *somewhere* to go, somewhere where Logan *wasn't*, while she processed whatever had just happened.

What *had* just happened? She'd been so overcome with joy from Logan's news that she'd almost *hugged* him! What on earth? First of all, she'd known that news was coming, so why did it elate her so? Had it been the look of joy on Logan's face? Had his joy been contagious? And second, even if she did have a good reason to be overjoyed, she didn't need to go around hugging other songwriters—especially not *Logan Hawkins*. Good grief! What would he have thought? He would've thought she was into him or something. She tried to laugh at the preposterousness of this thought, but her face didn't even crack a smile.

She ran a hand over her face as if to massage it into action. What was going on? She turned on the water and began to wash her hands. *It's no big deal*, she told herself. She'd helped another artist out of a creative jam. Her efforts had paid off. They'd created something good together, something that another artist had validated. That's all. *That's* why she'd been so happy. It hadn't really had anything to do with Logan. What a relief. She turned the water off and looked in the mirror. *I just need to get some sleep*, she told herself, even though she didn't feel tired.

She left the bathroom, thanking God again that it hadn't been her to find the spider drawing on her toilet paper and returned to her office. She had emails to answer. Several people had asked her to cowrite with them, and she had procrastinated with turning them down. She didn't want to hurt their feelings, but she just didn't like cowriting. She'd tried it with several artists, but each of them had wanted to quit when the song was "good enough." That wasn't how Hannah operated. She wouldn't call herself a perfectionist, exactly, but she always wanted to give every song her best.

She wiggled her mouse to wake up her computer screen. She was going to answer these emails right now, because there would be an onslaught of them when people heard she'd cowritten with Logan. Might as well get the first wave out of the way before the second wave hit.

Her screen remained dark. She wiggled the mouse again. Oh great, computer problems. She was so *not* a techie. She checked to make sure that her computer was on, and it was. The screen was turned on. It just wouldn't wake up. She groaned and pushed her chair back. She would have to ask Alex.

As she headed down the hall, she could hear Logan in the kitchen, telling someone about his spider gag. Did he ever work? She rolled her eyes and knocked on Alex's door. Alex quickly beckoned her inside. "What's up?"

"I can't get my computer screen to stop sleeping." She cringed at her lack of technical vocabulary.

Alex pushed her chair away from the desk. "Let's take a look."

Feeling like an imbecile, Hannah followed the office manager back down the hallway. Over Alex's shoulder, Hannah saw Logan step out of the kitchen—smiling. He was up to something. Again. She hoped it didn't involve her as she stepped back into her own office and made sure to shut the door. It was bad enough she couldn't turn on her computer. She didn't need Logan hearing about it.

Alex sat down in Hannah's chair and jiggled her mouse, just as Hannah had done two minutes ago, and nothing happened. Hannah sighed in relief. Sometimes when she asked for help with electronics, the helper just touched the thing and the problem was solved. That was super annoying. She'd once called a tow truck and the driver had wiggled a single wire, given her a patronizing look, and then driven away from her and her perfectly operational vehicle parked on the shoulder for no reason.

Alex flipped Hannah's mouse over.

"The batteries are good," Hannah said. "I replaced them not long ago."

Alex looked up at her, and she looked amused.

Immediately, Hannah felt defensive.

"It's not the batteries." Alex scraped her fingernail across the bottom of the mouse. "It appears that someone has played a small prank on you."

Hannah groaned before she even understood what she was groaning at. Logan. Again. "What kind of prank?"

Alex looked at her as though she were dumb. "No big deal." She almost sounded defensive of Logan and his antics. Of course she did. Everyone loved Logan. "He just put some masking tape on top of the little light, so your mouse didn't know it was moving." She returned the mouse to its pad and jiggled it, and of course, the computer screen sprang to life.

It was the tow truck driver all over again.

"Thanks, Alex," Hannah mumbled. It wasn't that she was ungrateful. She was embarrassed.

"Don't mention it." Alex got out of Hannah's chair and headed for the door. When she opened it, Logan almost fell into the room.

"Hey!" he cried out with too much joviality. "I was just about to knock! What's going on?"

Alex laughed as though he was hilarious and then left the room.

Logan stood there looking at Hannah as if waiting for praise.

"I think you know what's going on in here."

He still played dumb.

Fine. She wasn't going to give him the satisfaction. She sat and spun the chair toward her desk, putting her hand on the problematic mouse. "Absolutely nothing is going on in here, and I wish you'd go back to your work and let me do mine."

He didn't answer. Had he left? Should she look to make sure? Or was he standing there staring at the back of her head? If he was, then she certainly wasn't going to give him the satisfaction of turning to look at him. So she wouldn't. She would just live with the uncertainty. If he was still standing there, he would toddle off eventually. She opened her email app and then clicked on the first unanswered message.

The words popped onto the screen, and she tried to read them, but she couldn't retain what she was reading. She read the first sentence at least four times before giving up. He wasn't still standing there, was he? Of course not. It had been too long now. So she should just check to make sure.

She tried to be sneaky as she looked over her shoulder at the doorway, which, blessedly, stood empty. Oh good, he'd left. Now she could focus on the task at hand.

But why was she a little disappointed?

Chapter 8

On the way to the animal hospital, Logan tried to distract his mind by coming up with new ways to mess with Hannah. Golly, she was fun. He'd been afraid that tape on her mouse would be too obvious, but it wasn't. Not for Hannah.

But try as he might, he couldn't come up with another good gag. He'd felt kind of bad after the spider in the bathroom, and ended up glad that Chloe had been the one to discover it. He didn't really want to *scare* Hannah. *Startle* her, yes, but with Hannah, there was a fine line between scare and startle. He had to be careful.

And he certainly didn't want to do anything to hurt her feelings. He never wanted to hurt *anyone's* feelings, and certainly not hers. He wanted to make her *laugh*—not upset her.

So he couldn't put salt in her sugar shaker, because that was too mean. And did Hannah even use sugar in her coffee? Somehow, he didn't think so. And he couldn't Photoshop a picture of her head onto the body of her least favorite country superstar wearing a skimpy gown. He'd been really tempted by that one, as he knew Hannah would be horrified to be even virtually attached to something that racy—but it didn't feel right. Neither did hiding a snake in her desk drawer or covering her door knob with slime or putting a giant fake insect on the inside of her lampshade—all fantastic pranks he'd pulled in the past. But those weren't for Hannah.

Hannah was different.

He pulled his truck into the hospital parking lot, gave up on the mental search, and parked. But as he slid out of his truck, it came to him—the *best* Hannah prank yet. His whole body felt lighter at the thought of it. Yes, he would do it as soon as possible.

As soon as he stepped through the front door and was hit by the air conditioning and the smell of antiseptic, the lightness left him, replaced by a hefty dread. He stepped up to the counter, but he didn't need to identify himself. They knew who he was. He tried to smile, tried to be charming, tried to flirt with the familiar pretty face that greeted him, but he knew his efforts were weak. His charm currently had no verve. *I still have to write the verve song*, he reminded himself.

"You can come on back," the pretty face said.

He followed her through some swinging doors, and the antiseptic smell grew stronger. Logan caught sight of Otis asleep in a kennel, and a lump formed in his throat. This was so unfair. Dr. Dewitt appeared beside the kennel and held out his hand. "Hi, Logan."

Logan shook his hand, but didn't say anything. He didn't trust himself to speak.

The doctor avoided eye contact, giving Logan a layer of privacy he sorely needed. He was afraid his eyes were going to start leaking again. The doc unlocked Otis's kennel and keeping his eyes on the dog, said, "He seemed to tolerate this treatment better." He reached in and scratched Otis's head. "I think we might have finally found the best combination for the little guy."

Otis stirred, and Logan stepped closer. He wanted his best friend to be able to see him when he woke up. "Hey there, bud." Otis's tail flicked, and Logan's heart leapt at that almost-wag. He hadn't been wagging at all after the first chemotherapy treatment—he'd almost died. The doctors couldn't explain it; Otis had simply had a bad reaction to the drugs.

"Go ahead," Dr. Dewitt said gently. "You can take him if you don't mind carrying him out. He'll still be groggy for a while. We had to give him a sedative so he wouldn't take the IV out, but he should be fine." He finally looked at Logan. "If you don't want to carry him, you're welcome to hang out for a while until he comes to."

"Oh, no, I can carry him." He hadn't been hesitating because he wasn't willing to carry his dog out of the building. He'd just been reluctant to disturb him. Otis actually looked comfortable for the first time in weeks. He stepped forward and slid one arm under his dog and then gently scooped him into his chest. He suddenly couldn't wait to get his friend home and onto the couch, under the covers where he belonged. "Thank you," he said to the doctor and turned toward the door.

"You can use the back door." He gestured toward a glass door in the other direction. "It's a bit more private that way. And let me know how he's feeling tomorrow, or, if there's trouble before that, give me a call."

The lump in Logan's throat tried to make a comeback. He was overwhelmed with gratitude. He nodded at the good doctor and then headed for the secret exit.

Chapter 9

Thanks to a pesky dentist appointment, which she'd already managed to postpone three times, Hannah was an hour late to work on Thursday morning. The house was abuzz with activity. Apparently, Cole Washburne was so impressed with Logan and Hannah's joint effort that he wanted to hear more songs from Platinum Publishing. This was good news, of course, but Hannah felt it more like a tidal wave of pressure. She hurried to her office, wondering why the door was shut, and turned the doorknob intent on barging in—but the door didn't give much. It opened, sure, about two inches, and then bounced back at her as if someone on the inside had pushed it shut with the exact same amount of force she had exerted.

What on earth? From down the hall came a snicker, and then another snicker from a deeper throat.

Oh. Of course. *Logan.*

She turned to glare at the peanut gallery, but they'd already ducked back into the kitchen, or wherever they were lurking. She tried to push the door open again, more slowly this time, and heard a weird creaking sound. She peeked in through the two-inch crack to see what she could see and was startled to find information right in front of her face. It took her a second to process that information, though. What exactly was she looking at so close to her eyeballs? Why was something bright red suspended right in front of her face? And why was something bright yellow hanging just beneath it? And she smelled something—a scent so overwhelmingly familiar, she felt like an utter dope being unable to identify it.

Then all the information coalesced into a theory that made sense: balloons.

But wait. How were a few balloons preventing her from entering her own office?

The snickers came again and she almost growled. Whatever this was, she didn't have time for it. Cole Washburne wanted songs. "What did you do?" she called into the empty hallway.

"I didn't do anything!" Chloe called back, and then Logan laughed again.

She wanted to kill him. "Logan! I'm serious! I need to get into my office!" She pushed on the door with her hip and it gave a little more, just before a loud *bang* nearly made her jump out of her skin. Was someone shooting at her? Nope. Balloons popped, didn't they? She was thankful that this gave her an idea. She fumbled around in her purse for her keys and then found the longest one—the one to her parents' garage—and then stuck it through the crack. At first, nothing happened, and she stabbed harder at the bright red pain-in-the-butt balloon until another *bang* sounded. She jumped again, even though she'd been expecting it, but this explosion gave her an odd satisfaction, and she was eager to pop a third balloon, and then a fourth, and then a fifth. It sounded like front row at the Fourth of July fireworks. The door gave way some more, and she was able to see that her entire office was stuffed full of balloons, from about waist-high to ceiling. She went to work, stabbing at them one by one like an overeager ninja with a two-short sword. *Good grief, this must have cost him a fortune.*

Finally, after she had slaughtered about thirty balloons (she'd lost count) and pressed her body into the room, Logan materialized behind her. "Need some help?"

She didn't gratify him by turning around. "Don't flatter yourself." *Bang.* She kept stabbing and jabbing. Her floor was littered with latex confetti. *Bang.*

"You don't have to pop them *all*. Maybe some of us would like some balloons in our office." He made it sound as though she were eating all the office candy at Halloween.

Bang. "Fine. Take what you want before I pop it."

He started pulling balloons out of the cluster of balloons, and when he did, they all shifted, and the one her garage key was aiming at scooted toward safety. *How annoying.* "Why did you do this?" she snapped. *Why did I ask that?* It didn't matter *why* Logan did anything. He probably didn't even have a reason. He was a child. *Bang. Bang.*

He handed several balloons through her door to Chloe, who disappeared with them. Then he reached up to grab some more. Her desk appeared in front of her. They were making progress. *Bang.*

"I wanted to make you laugh," he mumbled.

What? He thought this would make her *laugh?* Was he that dumb? She hadn't thought so. *Bang.* Her arm was growing tired. She considered switching to her left hand, but she wasn't sure how graceful that would look, and Logan was watching.

She collapsed onto the stool in front of her electric piano and glared at him. "I'll pop the rest of these later. I've got to get to work."

She couldn't see his facial expression, but she sensed he was disappointed. "I can get them out of here for you. You go ahead and write."

"You do know that Cole Washburne wants more songs?"

"Washburne can wait another ten minutes."

She turned on her keyboard. She wasn't sure that was true. There was a city full of songwriters champing at the bit to deliver Cole's next hit. Ten minutes could make a difference of thousands of dollars. In fact, ten seconds could make that difference. She took out a fresh sheet of paper and then played a riff that had been running through her head. She could feel his eyes on her and suddenly felt bad that she'd been so snippy with him. But how was she supposed to react? He'd come into *her* personal space and taken up *her* personal time with his foolishness. If she was nice about it, he'd just keep it up.

He carried an armload of balloons out of her office, and she got to work.

Forty minutes later, she realized two things: he'd never come back for another armload; and she had to go to the bathroom. Grudgingly, she left her stool with the intent to hurry. She had half a new chorus written, and she didn't want to lose the flow.

She was just about to enter the ladies' room when she heard her name. She stopped in her tracks and strained to hear. It sounded like Chloe's voice coming from Logan's office. She furtively took a few steps in that direction, and then she heard Alex's voice too. What, were they having a staff meeting in there?

"Why did you do balloons, dude?" Alex said. "That's a lot of work."

"I thought it would be funny." Logan sounded sad.

"It *is* funny," Chloe said. Of course. Chloe thought everything Logan did was funny. If Chloe didn't have a husband and three kids, Hannah would think she had the hots for Logan.

She turned to go back to the bathroom. They were discussing the balloons. Not interesting.

"I was trying to make her laugh," Logan said. "I wanted a prank that wouldn't make me a jerk. Just something innocent."

"Since when do you care about being a jerk?" Chloe asked.

Logan mumbled something, but Hannah couldn't make it out. She crept closer.

"I get that you didn't want to upset her," Alex said, "but then why prank her at all? Just leave her alone. She's obviously no fun."

"She's fun," Logan said quickly. He paused. "Sometimes."

"If you say so," Alex said.

Hannah, her cheeks burning, didn't hear anything after that and she feared she was missing something, so she stepped even closer. Hence, she was in perfect position for Chloe to smash into her when she came flying out of Logan's office. "Ahh!" she cried out, and Hannah wanted to die.

"What?" Alex stepped out into the hall to see Chloe holding onto Hannah's arms to steady her from falling, assistance that Hannah did not need or want.

She shook herself free from Chloe's hands. "Sorry." She wheeled away, her face so hot she was sure there must be flames.

"Eavesdrop much?" Alex called after her. Her tone was too playful to offend, but even if it hadn't been, Hannah didn't have the energy to be offended. She was too busy being embarrassed.

Chapter 10

Logan couldn't remember the last time he'd felt so horrible. It had been at least forever. He was a jolly guy.

But he'd upset Hannah, and then she'd run into Chloe in the hallway, and now she'd been squirreled away in her office for hours. She hadn't even come out for lunch. True, she never ate lunch with the rest of them, always claiming to be too busy, but she at least popped out to get something out of the fridge or use the microwave.

He gently knocked on her door.

There was no response.

Half expecting it to be locked, he turned the knob and the door fell open. Hannah sat at her keyboard with her back to him.

"Sorry to interrupt ..." He wasn't sure what to say next, so he stopped.

She did nothing to acknowledge his presence.

He quietly shut the door behind him and then went and sat in her office chair, so that he was only a few feet away from her and looking at the side of her face. Her profile was distinctive—beautiful. He'd never noticed that before. He took a deep breath.

She finally looked at him. Her eyes were puffy and red.

"I'm really sorry," he said. "I honestly was just trying to do a good thing."

She nodded slowly. "I know. I just think your sense of humor is very different from mine."

Yeah, he thought, *I have one.* He thought it best not to express that aloud. "I'll get the rest of the balloons out of here soon. I just wanted to give you some space, because I knew you were angry."

She looked up at the many balloons still stacked under the ceiling. "You can leave them for a while. They're growing on me." She slid her eyes toward him. "And I'm not mad so much as embarrassed. I'm sorry I was eavesdropping—"

He held up one hand. "No! Don't be sorry. We were talking about you. Of *course* you were going to try to hear what we were saying. Any of us would have done that." He leaned toward her. "You know, we're kind of a family around here, so it's really no big deal. Don't be embarrassed."

She didn't look comforted. He had the urge to hug her. Of course, he didn't. He'd seen what she could do with that giant key, and didn't want her to turn it on him.

He slapped his legs and stood up. "All right, didn't mean to interrupt your genius. Just wanted to apologize."

She sniffed. "It's okay. But really, Logan, can we please stop with the pranks? I'm just not a prank person."

He sat back down. He didn't know how to answer that. "I guess?" He stared at her, waiting for a response. "You don't think *any* of them are funny, ever?"

She shook her head. "Sorry. Not my thing. And think of the time you'd have to write if you didn't spend all your time taping people's mouses—"

"Mice," he interrupted, sure that would get a smile out of her.

"Huh?" She wasn't laughing.

"Never mind. Go on."

"Right. Well, you say we're a family, so let me speak frankly, as one relative to another. Logan, you're a talented songwriter. Think of how many more hits you'd have under your belt if you just applied yourself, if you'd make better use of your time."

He was back to being berated by his high school English teacher. That woman had given him similar speeches, and he'd thought she was a nag. He didn't want to think that about Hannah. "You know, Hannah, there's more to life than time management."

She gave him a blank look that seemed to say, *There is?*

He suddenly felt very sorry for her. "Yes, I'm pretty good at this gig, but in the great scheme of things, who cares? And you're super talented too, but again, in the scope of the universe, what does it matter? We're only on this earth for a little while, so why not relax and try to enjoy it?"

As he talked, her expression slowly morphed from clueless to irritated.

Maybe I should stop talking. He clamped his mouth shut.

She rolled her shoulders back. "I enjoy life."

He had never seen any evidence to support that. "Good. I'm glad. I worry about you because you're always so tightly wound. I wish you'd stop and smell the roses every once in a while."

Her expression made it clear that she wanted no more life advice from him, and he was suddenly tired of trying to talk to someone who wasn't hearing a word he was saying. "Okay then." He stood up again, this time intent on leaving. "Have a good rest of your day."

"You too."

He opened the door to find Alex standing there with her hand poised to knock. "There you are! Your dog sitter just called. Something's wrong with Otis."

Chapter 11

Hannah watched Logan leave her office, and whispered a prayer for his dog. She didn't have time for a dog, herself, but she was a dog lover. She'd always had them growing up, and she knew the pain of losing one. She hoped that wasn't happening with Logan's dog. She'd never met Otis, but she'd seen pictures of him in Logan's office, and he was a cute little guy.

She turned back toward her work station and heaved a great sigh. She knew that she was tightly wound. She didn't need to be told so by the likes of Logan Hawkins. Stop and smell the roses. What a bunch of drivel. What a cliché. Sure, it had been a hit song a zillion years ago, but it also sounded like something she'd find in a fortune cookie, or something her grandmother would stitch into her embroidery hoop.

And she didn't even agree with the sentiment. Life was too short to spend it sniffing roses, unless one was really into roses. An idea popped into her head. What if she wrote a song about *not* stopping to smell the roses? A song about working hard and getting ahead and making the most of every moment. Her brain began to spin with possibilities, and she pulled out a fresh sheet of paper.

The ideas gushed out of her, and her pen hustled to keep up. This wasn't usually how she worked. Usually, the melody came first, but she wasn't going to argue with the muse. She wrote, "Yes, life is short. That's why we shouldn't waste it." Waste it on what? She started a list: television, drugs, video games, cell phone games, arguing, social media, crushes on people who would never be who you thought they were and would never return the feelings ... her pen couldn't keep up. Before she'd even finished the list, she'd started listing what *does* matter in life: success, work ethic, leaving a legacy behind, accomplishment, validation, making a difference, making the world a better place than it was when you got here ... Soon, a chorus started taking shape:

I don't have time for stopping

The clock is tick tock hopping

Those roses can bloom without me

Gotta get to the door before it closes

Don't have time to smell the roses

Cole Washburne was *not* going to want to record this song. That was okay, though. Because Maggie Hammer could turn it into the single of the year. Hannah's knees bounced up and down as she kept writing, already humming the melody in her head.

When she had a page full of words, circles, and arrows, she paused to massage her right hand and look down at her paper. Then she began to pull pieces out of the chaos and form them into a verse. *Time is of the essence, a limited supply ... close your eyes tonight, and the seconds say goodbye ... They never come back, long gone, all spent, a hundred percent. So seize the moment, seize the day, every minute matters, that's the only way ...* She launched into the chorus with enough gusto that the whole building could hear her. She didn't care. She spun on her stool toward the keyboard and started to play the notes, unable to remember when she'd been this excited about a song.

It was funny, too, because she almost always wrote ballads. But the more she worked on this song, the faster the tempo got. She was really rocking it! Her keyboard might be wondering if she was possessed. Just for kicks, she turned on the drum accompaniment and turned up the volume, suddenly envisioning her song on a high school basketball team's warm-up playlist.

Maybe she should have Logan fill her office up with balloons more often, if it led to this sort of productiveness. Maybe she'd been rash to ask him for no more pranks. Apparently, pranks could lead to good things. She smiled at the thought of Logan and his ridiculous balloons, and she sang her first verse again.

An hour later, she had finished the song. It was, by a giant margin, the fastest she'd ever finished a song. Feeling entirely wrung out, she began shutting off all her electronics so that she could head home for the night.

As she passed by Suzette's office, she noticed the light was still on. "You're here late," Hannah said, a little concerned.

"Yes! I was listening to your new creation." Suzette strolled toward the door, and Hannah could see multiple balloons dotting her ceiling. "I love that melody. I think you might have another winner. Color me impressed."

Hannah put her purse strap over her shoulder. "Thanks. Hey, you haven't heard any updates on Logan's dog have you?"

Suzette's eyes widened a little. "Not tonight, no. He's got cancer, I know that."

Hannah's stomach plummeted.

"It's a new diagnosis, and they're fighting it, because the dog's so young, but he already has epilepsy, so I'm not sure what's happening. Logan's being pretty tight-lipped about it."

Hannah couldn't imagine Logan being tight-lipped about anything. "Maybe, just while the dog's sick, he could come to work with Logan? Then Logan wouldn't need a dog-sitter?"

Suzette's surprise deepened. "Maybe," she said slowly. "Let me think about that. And you let me know when you're ready to pitch that song to someone."

"I'm ready," Hannah said quickly.

"My, my! You are just full of surprises today. Are you sure? No endless tweaking and polishing till it's perfect?"

Hannah considered that for a second. "No, I think it's ready."

"Well, I'll be ..." Suzette tipped her head to the side and smiled at her, as if she was gazing at a child she was particularly proud of. "All right. We can start tomorrow."

"Maggie Hammer gets first dibs."

"Yes, ma'am."

Chapter 12

By the time Logan arrived at the dog-sitter's apartment, which was directly underneath his, Otis's seizure was long since over, and he was back to his old self. His medication was supposed to prevent seizures, but Dr. Dewitt had taken him off one of his drugs until he was done with chemotherapy.

Now, Logan sat on his couch with Otis sleeping soundly beside him, seeming to feel fine without a care in the world. This was okay, as Logan was worrying enough for the both of them.

The dog-sitter had announced that she would no longer be able to watch Otis. The seizure had freaked her out, and she said he was just too much for her now. This wasn't the end of the world, as Logan didn't think Otis was too fond of her anyway, but Logan wasn't sure what to do with him. Otis was a rescue dog with a history of aggression, so doggy daycares wouldn't take him, even though he hadn't shown *any* aggression in the years that Logan had had him. Logan sighed, wishing he'd lied to the daycares and said Otis had never even shown his teeth.

Grudgingly, he picked up his phone to text Suzie Q and tell her that he wouldn't be in to the office the next day, even though it was Friday and she would assume he was just trying to game a long weekend. He'd done it before, so he couldn't blame her for jumping to conclusions. But he had to figure out what to do with Otis before he could go to work. He didn't want to leave him home alone in his condition.

Suzie Q responded immediately. "Bring him into work. He can stay in your office, if you can clear a spot for him."

Logan's mouth fell open. He couldn't believe it. Seriously? Where had this come from? Instantly, he thought of Hannah. She would so *not* be impressed with this. He'd never asked her, but he would bet the farm that she wasn't a dog lover. "Are you sure it will be okay with my fellow songsmiths?" he texted.

"Sure. I checked with Chloe. And it was Hannah's idea."

He almost fell off the couch. That couldn't possibly be true, could it? "Okay, thank you," he wrote. "You have no idea how much I appreciate that." And he did. His whole body relaxed at the idea. If they played their cards right, Otis could come to work with him for the rest of his life, even after he'd gotten better. Logan just had to write a few more number one hits, so he could become more indispensable to Suzie Q. He kicked off his boots and grabbed an afghan. He squeezed himself between the back of the couch and sleeping Otis's warm back, and then unfolded the blanket to cover them both up. He hated how much weight Otis had lost and ran a hand down his soft back. He let his hand rest there and used the other hand to grab the remote. He knew he was going to fall asleep soon, but he liked to drift off to reruns of *Cheers*. There was just something soothing about Norm Peterson's voice.

He was sound asleep in seconds and soon he was dreaming of a field of roses. They seemed to be of every color, even weird non-rose colors like orange, turquoise, and lavender. The flowers stretched as far as he could see in every direction, and to his right, several hundred feet away, he saw Hannah. Her hair flowed down her back in giant dark curls, and she wore a long, sleeveless pink dress that perfectly matched the pink roses. Then he knew he was dreaming. Hannah wouldn't wear her hair down, wouldn't wear a dress like that, and certainly wouldn't be standing in a field of roses.

He hollered her name, but she didn't look at him. She reached down and plucked a rose from the ground, and he thought about warning her about thorns, but all at once he realized these dream-roses didn't have thorns. She sniffed the flower and smiled. Then she bent to pick another. He started walking toward her, watching her as she picked one flower after another. Though she had nearly a dozen in her hands by now, she had yet to duplicate a color. He picked up his pace, and then realized that, though he was moving, he wasn't getting any closer to her. This realization saddened him, and he stopped walking.

He looked down and saw that Otis was there beside him, eating rose petals. He laughed and reached down to pat his best friend's head, and when he looked back up, Hannah was gone. And his chest ached with missing her.

Chapter 13

Alex didn't give Hannah a chance to shut the front door behind her on Sunday morning before telling her that Logan had brought his dog to work. She made the news sound scandalous. Hannah's first thought was that she couldn't believe that Logan had beaten her to work, but once she recovered from that jolt, she had time to be excited about the idea of a pooch in the building. Alex's pinched face made it clear that she didn't share Hannah's joy. Hannah left Alex behind and made a beeline for the smallest office so she could meet the pup.

But Suzette stopped her on her way. "Do you want me to send the song to Maggie, or do you want to do it?"

This option normally wouldn't be offered, but Hannah already had a relationship with Maggie. "I'll do it. I'll do it today. Right after I—"

"Meet the dog? Yes"—Suzette stepped out of the way and swept her arm down to invite Hannah to pass by—"I agree with your priorities."

Hannah brushed past Suzette and approached Logan's room with a giddiness distinctly unlike her. Was she really this excited to see a dog? As she neared the door, she heard voices, and at first thought it must be Logan talking to his four-legged friend, an image that endeared him to her. But when she pushed on the door, it swung open to reveal a blond woman sitting cross-legged on the floor beside a dog bed: Willow. Hannah couldn't even see the dog, a fact that catapulted her into an unreasonable indignation.

"Hannah!" Logan jumped out of his chair, obviously delighted to see her. "Come on in! What a treat, having two beautiful women in my office." He smiled down at his dog, whom Hannah still couldn't see. "Look at you, Otis, attracting all the ladies."

Hannah's legs threatened to bolt, but some part of her knew that fleeing the scene would be embarrassing. She stepped into the room and glanced down at the dog bed, at the cutest little dog she'd ever seen peering up at her with giant brown eyes. Hannah had seen pictures of him on Logan's bulletin board, but he was much cuter in real life. He was almost all black, with just a hint of gray around his muzzle. He looked like a skinny French bulldog. Despite herself, she let out a small squeal of delight. She would've crouched to shower him with affection, but Willow was crowding her out. She looked at Logan, "What breed is he, again?"

Logan smiled broadly and held his hands out to his side with his palms up. "No idea." He still stood beside his chair, as if waiting for her to sit in it.

Of course, she was going to do no such thing. She started thinking of ways to politely leave the room. "Well, he's incredibly cute." She smiled at Willow. "Nice to see you again," she lied, and turned to go.

"Are you okay?"

She turned back toward Logan, who actually looked concerned.

"Yeah," she stammered, "just a little worried about the little guy." This wasn't a lie. It wasn't the whole truth about what was annoying her so much, but it wasn't a lie. What *was* annoying her so much, anyway? Logan was allowed to have a female visitor in his office. Willow was allowed to be there, Hannah told herself.

"Well, Otis and I appreciate the concern." Logan's voice was level, sober—a tone she wasn't used to coming from him. "But don't worry. He's going to be fine. He's got years and years left to live."

Really? Hannah looked down at the dog, doubt etched on her brow. As soon as she realized how obviously she was wearing that emotion, she tried to wipe it away.

But it was too late. Logan chuckled humorlessly. "Don't let his gray hairs fool you. He's done some hard living, but his doc says he's only about seven. So yes, years and years."

Hannah didn't know if he was trying to convince her, Otis, or himself, but she forced a smile and nodded. "Good then." She turned to go, beyond annoyed that Willow wouldn't let her near the dog. "If you need any help with him, let me know."

"Thank you!" Logan sounded surprised at her offer, and grateful.

"Oh, me too," Willow cooed. "I love dogs so much."

Hannah was already out in the hallway when Willow finished this declaration, so there was no one there to see her roll her eyes. She didn't know why Willow bothered her so much. She seemed innocuous enough, yet Hannah couldn't get away from her fast enough.

Hannah got another cup of coffee and then squirreled herself away in her office, trying to focus on work and not what was happening at the end of the hall. She truly was worried about the dog. It was good that Logan had such a positive attitude, but the dog was really sick. She hoped that Logan wasn't going to lose him. She could tell by the way Logan looked at the dog how much he loved him.

She shook her head, trying to will herself to focus. She played through her new song—which she'd titled, "No Time for Roses"—several times, and then recorded it. If they were going to shop it around, she would record it in a studio, but she was just sending it to Maggie Hammer, who would get the gist of it without needing to hear a studio version. And she had no doubt Maggie would cut the song, so she wasn't worried about being professional. She was more worried, like always, about not letting the grass grow under her feet while she messed around in the studio.

She uploaded the song to her cloud, and then wrote Maggie a short email and sent her the link. Then she sat back, feeling accomplished. She and Maggie Hammer had made each other a lot of money. In fact, Maggie had gotten one of Hannah's songs nominated for the Country Music Association's Song of the Year. It hadn't won, but that was okay. Hannah knew *why* it hadn't won, and it wasn't because of the song. Maggie's entry into the country music world had been laced with drama, and some of Nashville's pillars wanted to punish her for it. Maggie, however, wasn't worried about what the pillars thought. Her fans adored her, and they would adore her even more once she released "No Time for Roses." Hannah just knew it.

Chapter 14

Logan had tried everything he could think of to get Willow out of his office. Sure, she was a woman, and she was pretty, but he really wasn't in the mood, and he wanted Otis to rest. But Willow just wouldn't leave him alone. She wasn't taking any hints. He'd even said that *he* had to leave his office, but then she'd offered to stay behind and hang out with the dog.

Finally, he stopped trying to be tactful. "Willow, I'm sorry, but I've just remembered that I have a deadline coming up." This was not true. He never had deadlines. He didn't believe in them. "And I need to get to work right now." She stared at him, a vapid look in her eyes. "So, I need you to go, so that I can get to work." How much plainer could he make it?

Her eyes widened with sudden understanding. "Oh!"

He couldn't tell if she was offended. She looked down at the dog. "Do you want me to take Otis with me?"

What? Why would he want her to take his dog?

"So that he doesn't distract you?" she clarified.

"No," Logan said quickly and firmly, maybe too firmly. "He won't distract me."

She still didn't get up from the floor.

He stood and walked to the door. "Thanks for stopping by, though."

She finally stirred. "Oh, of course! When I saw you carry this cute little bundle of joy in, I just had to come visit!"

He made a mental note to sneak in the back door next time.

She managed to look graceful as she came to a standing position. He didn't know how she'd accomplished that. He always looked like a gompy old man whenever he tried to come out of the criss-cross applesauce position. Hence, he hadn't allowed himself to get *into* that position since the sixth grade.

She stopped and stood in the doorway, looking up at him. Her eyes were emerald green and really very pretty. So were her pink lips. Why was she staring at him? What was she waiting for? He smiled. She smiled back. "I would like to see you again soon, Logan. Would you like to come over after work? We're having a small get-together."

Of course they were. The Purple Oasis was always having a small get-together. But why would she think he could do that tonight? Didn't she see that he had a dog to care for? He'd only been able to hang out with her the other night because Otis had been spending the night at the animal hospital, and he'd told her that. "I don't think so."

Her face fell in disappointment, and she leaned her body into his, almost knocking him off balance. "Okay then," she said, her voice low and sultry, "maybe some other time."

"Yeah, maybe," he said, because he didn't know what else to say.

She finally left, throwing him one more flirtatious look over her bare, tan shoulder.

He shut the door behind her and leaned against it, looking down at Otis, who seemed to be saying, "Thank you for getting rid of her" with his eyes. Or maybe Logan was just projecting his own emotions onto the dog. He'd been guilty of that before.

He returned to his office chair and looked at the blank page of his notebook. It was supposed to contain song lyrics, deadline or no deadline. Maybe he should write a song about not liking his neighbor, even though she was gorgeous. He picked up his pencil. But why *didn't* he like his neighbor? She was obviously into him. Maybe it was just the timing. Maybe he was too focused on Otis right now to think about women. Nah, he didn't think that was it. He put the pencil down. He didn't want to write about Willow.

Then he had a new idea, and it came to him so fast and so clearly that he couldn't believe he hadn't thought of it earlier. It was like an instant download from the cloud of the muse, and his pencil flew across the page. Sure, the theme had been covered before in country music, but not in decades, and besides, if there was one thing the country music culture could endure, it was repetition.

There are fields and fields of them, if you will only look, he wrote. He could tell this was going to be a ballad, which was different for him. He usually wrote up-tempo rockabilly tunes. *When you hurry to the end, you miss all the pages* ... Otis wagged his tail, as if appreciating the lyrics he hadn't heard yet. With a tremendous feeling of accomplishment, Logan penned the last two lines of his new chorus: *Smile, slow down, take notice — and stop and smell the roses.*

Chapter 15

Hannah knew she was behaving neurotically, but she couldn't help it. No matter how she tried to punish or incentivize herself, she couldn't seem to make her finger stop hitting the refresh button on her email inbox. But no matter how many times she hit the button, nothing of consequence changed. Maggie Hammer still hadn't answered her.

It had been days.

She could see that Maggie, or at least someone rooting around in Maggie's inbox, had clicked on the link and downloaded the song. Her cloud account told her that much. But then—nothing.

Yesterday, Hannah had listened to her recording, just to make sure there wasn't a giant belch, or some other deterrent, in the middle of the recording, but there wasn't. She supposed there was a *possibility* that Maggie wouldn't like the song, but Hannah didn't think that was likely. The song was tight. Sure, she hadn't let anyone else hear it, except what they could hear through the walls, and artistically speaking, this wasn't wise.

When she was much younger, a song had woken her up in the middle of the night. She'd leapt out of bed to sing it into her voice recorder so that she wouldn't forget it. Then she'd gone back to bed and slept like a baby after a milk binge. In the morning, she'd excitedly played it for her mentor, who had said, "I can see why this seemed brilliant at three in the morning, but alas, the sun must come up." At the time, she'd been crushed. Now, she laughed about that memory: in part, because she was so wildly more successful than that mentor had ever been; and in part because it was a good lesson to learn: never trust one's conception of brilliance when evaluating one's own work.

Yet, here she was doing it again. But she was so *sure* this time. No way was she misjudging this one. Still, she should probably get a second opinion. Oddly, her first thought was Logan. She should ask him what he thought of it. It was his style of song anyway, and reaping praise from him would feel wonderful. She blinked. It would, wouldn't it? But why? Why was she suddenly craving his validation? She didn't know, but the idea was so foreign that she decided *not* to ask his opinion.

A peal of laughter shot down the hallway and through Hannah's closed door. That sounded like Alex, who wasn't a big laugher. Something must *really* be funny. She opened her door and peeked out into the hallway. Her nose was greeted by the overwhelming smell of popcorn, and her mouth watered. She didn't even like microwaved popcorn, but it sure did smell heavenly. More giggling came from the kitchen, and she heard the low rumble of Logan's voice.

Curiosity beckoned her out of her office and down the hallway toward the kitchen. Maybe she needed some plastic popcorn after all.

When she rounded the corner and came into the kitchen, there was popcorn all over the floor. Alex's face was pink from laughter, and she held her stomach as if trying to hold the rest of her giggles in. The sight of Hannah sent her into another fit, however, and more giggles erupted out of her.

Logan was grinning from ear to ear. "You're going to have to clean this up, Alex. I'd have Otis do it, but he's on a strict get-well-soon diet, so—"

"Diet?" Alex shriek-laughed. "Popcorn's good for you!"

Logan looked down at the floor. "It's not the popcorn. It's all the sugar."

And she was at it again, her head tipped back, her impressive voice box sending wails of laughter to the high ceiling. What on earth was going on here?

Logan was laughing too, and suddenly, Hannah felt left out. "What's so funny?" She folded her arms across her chest.

He looked at her, his eyes sparkling. "Sorry to interrupt your work, Hannah. I just played a little prank on Alex here."

Hannah's chest hurt. Sorry to interrupt her? So she was such a drudge that Logan just assumed she was toiling away alone in her office? This was true, of course. That's what she'd been doing. But he didn't need to call her out like that, basically saying, "We know you were working and *not* having fun, so we're so sorry we interrupted you with *our* fun, which we're totally having, by the way, *without* you." A small voice in Hannah's head suggested she was being irrational, but she shushed that voice straightaway.

The smile slid off Logan's face, a look of concern now in its place. "You okay, Hannah?"

She tried to force a perky smile. "Yes! Why is there popcorn all over the floor?"

"Oh for crying out loud, I'll clean it up," Alex said, as if Hannah was a giant taskmaster who was scolding her.

"No, no," Hannah tried to protest. "I'm not *upset* that there's popcorn on the floor. I just wanted to know what the prank was."

Logan and Alex exchanged a look and then started laughing again.

Hannah was about to give up. She wanted to hear about the prank, sure, but not this badly.

Finally, Logan spoke up. "You know how Alex eats *way* too much salt?"

Hannah had no idea about Alex's salt intake levels. She nodded. "Sure."

"Basically, on *everything*? No matter what she eats, she salts it first, *especially* her microwave popcorn, which she makes all the time, stinking up the entire house."

"It only stinks when I burn it," Alex protested.

Logan ignored this. "Anyway, I put sugar in her salt shaker." He snickered, and Alex started cackling again.

Sugar in the salt shaker? That was it? Was that really that funny?

Alex looked at her eagerly, as if she now couldn't wait to share. "I took a giant handful and shoved it into my mouth, and it was so sweet, I almost gagged. I couldn't imagine what was wrong with it. I thought I'd accidentally bought the wrong kind or something, but then I saw Logan laughing, and I just knew." She punched him in the shoulder playfully.

Hannah looked down at the floor, still not understanding why there was a carpet of maize.

"She was so pleased with my prank that she threw the bag of popcorn at me, and of course, because I'm agile like a cat, I stepped out of the way, and now Alex has to clean up a big mess." He waved at her as he started to walk toward Hannah. "Have fun. I've got to get back to Otis." He brushed by Hannah, and she caught a whiff of his aftershave over the popcorn smell. He smelled heavenly. She didn't think she'd ever noticed the smell of his aftershave before. Maybe he was wearing something new? She watched him leave the room and then gave Alex one more glance before leaving the room herself. Alex was staring down at the floor, looking sad, as if she had just realized that was her popcorn down there and now she had nothing to eat.

Hannah returned to her office feeling lonely. She didn't know why she was having this emotion in a house full of people. She never felt lonely. Even when she was alone, she was too busy to feel lonely. An accusing voice in her head spoke up: *You're jealous that Logan pulled a prank on someone else.* She laughed aloud. *That* was ridiculous. She was *not* jealous of anything to do with Logan, and she didn't like pranks. Still, that loneliness persisted.

She hit the refresh button again.

Chapter 16

Logan sat on the floor of his office with his notebook in his lap, stroking a sleeping Otis while trying to work on lyrics that *didn't* involve a dog. This was not easy to do when concern for his dog clouded his every thought. He'd done well distracting himself with the sugar on the popcorn gag, but now he was back to worrying.

On some level, he knew that Otis was just a dog, and that dogs didn't live forever. He knew he would survive losing Otis, but he sure wasn't ready to do that yet, and whenever that rational voice in his head tried to console him, his stronger emotional self would squash it like a bug: yes, Otis was a dog, but he was so much more than that. He was Logan's best friend, his partner, his confidant. Otis was more like an extension of Logan himself than he was a separate entity. Logan shook his head. He was so tired of thinking about this. He needed another prank.

Hannah. Hadn't she been weird about the popcorn thing? She'd almost seemed *sad* that he hadn't put sugar on *her* popcorn. This was absurd, of course. Hannah had made it clear that she didn't want any more pranks done in her honor, so surely she wasn't *jealous* of Alex? No way.

He sat down in his chair and rolled it toward his laptop. Maybe he should do a little something to Hannah, in case she *had* felt left out. Nah, he shouldn't. But he wanted to. It was like an addiction, and he was craving another dose.

Five minutes later, Logan had signed Hannah up for three email newsletters: how to live well with dentures; how to breed and sell goats; and one from a German knitting club. That last one was written in

German, so he hoped she'd have difficulty locating the unsubscribe button.

Feeling better, he went back to his notebook and wrote a few lines, but was soon interrupted by a very excited Suzie Q, who wanted him in her office *stat*. She used that word a lot. He suspected she binge-watched those hospital soap operas. He gave Otis another pat and then headed down the hall.

"Exciting news!" she said when he entered.

He'd figured that much. "What's up?"

She leaned forward and put her hands on her desk. "Branch Bronson wants to record your new song!" She said it as if she couldn't believe it.

A chill danced across Logan's shoulders. Branch Bronson? For real? "But ... but doesn't he only record his own songs?"

She shrugged. "Yes, usually, but it's been a while since he's had a number one. Maybe he feels like he needs some fresh blood?" She obviously had no idea why Branch Bronson was suddenly going to use someone else's song, and she just as obviously didn't care.

And who was he to look a gift horse in the mouth? "Yeah, I guess it doesn't matter why he wants it—he can sure have it!"

"I thought so, and I already told him as much. Well, I told his people, anyway. The paperwork is in the works. I just wanted to tell you. And I'll send someone out for cake. We're going to have a little celebration at five." She winked at him.

He stood there, frozen for a minute, and then turned to leave, still feeling as though he were floating above the floor. Then he had another thought and turned back. "Why did you even send it to him? Do you normally send him songs?"

It seemed she'd been expecting the question. "No, I sure don't. But I sent it out to everyone. It was a good song, and I cast a wide net. One of his people must have gotten an ear on it." She looked up at him. "Like you said, maybe we shouldn't question it too much. At least, not until the album drops." She winked again.

He didn't think he'd ever loved Suzie Q so much, even counting that brilliant moment when she'd first hired him.

Without consulting his brain, his feet carried him to Hannah's door. He couldn't wait to share his good news with her. Finding out if she had checked her inbox lately for new newsletter subscriptions would be a bonus. He knocked on the door.

"Come in!"

He opened the door, walked in as though he owned the place, and plopped down on her couch. "You aren't going to believe this."

She sat at her desk, with one hand glued to her mouse, a finger poised above it, looking ready to pounce. She looked at him and arched an eyebrow. "Oh, I believe it all right. And you do know that the denture toothpaste company newsletter was double opt in, right?"

He didn't know what this meant. "What?"

"Oh, don't play innocent with me. I know it was you. And I didn't confirm my subscription."

"Is that the only email you've gotten recently?" he baited her.

She scowled playfully. "Why, what else did you do?"

"I didn't do anything. Anyway, I came to tell you that my songwriting career has just reached its apex."

Her hand finally slid away from the mouse and she turned her whole body toward him. "What?" she said slowly.

"Yeah, it's only downhill from here." This was true. Sure, he might hit the summit again, but there would be no taller mountain.

"What, did Garth Brooks just cut one of your songs?" She knew how much he loved Garth. The posters in his office gave him away.

"Better. Branch Bronson."

The smile fell off her face. "No way."

"Yes way."

"But he doesn't sing other people's songs."

"I know."

They stared at each other for a minute, lost in the thrill of the news. He didn't detect one iota of jealousy from her, and he knew it wasn't there. She was ambitious, sure, the most ambitious person he'd ever met, but it was never at anyone else's expense. Hannah Carter only competed with herself; that competition was brutal enough.

"Wow, I can't believe it. Congratulations!"

"Thanks. We're going to have cake at five." He laughed, feeling foolish for being excited about cake when he had much bigger fish to fry.

"Which one?"

"Which cake? I don't know. Suzie Q is picking it, so it probably won't be very exciting. Probably vanilla with vanilla frosting, though I could put in a request for—"

"No, you imbecile, which *song*?"

"Oh." He chuckled. "Sorry. It's one you haven't heard. Brand-new. It's called 'Stop and Smell the Roses.'"

Chapter 17

Hannah's chest tightened so quickly that it physically hurt her. Her head got feverish, and beads of sweat broke out on the back of her neck.

"Are you okay?" Logan asked, actually managing to look concerned.

What could she say to that? Of course she wasn't okay! He didn't really think she would be, did he?" She opened her mouth, but no words came out.

He stood up and took a step toward her. She shrank away, her chair rolling back a few inches. He stopped. "Hannah, what is it?" His voice was soft now. It was hard to believe it was the voice of someone who had just driven a blade through her back. "You're pale. Are you feeling okay?" He was coming at her again, but her chair was up against her desk.

"I think you should go." Her voice sounded croaky.

He stopped and his whole body straightened. "Hannah, what is it? You can talk to me."

She couldn't believe how sweet he sounded. She had no idea he was such a good actor.

Her hands gripped her armrests so tightly that her fingers were starting to tingle. "Get out!" She tried to sound strong.

He didn't move.

Her eyes were wet with tears of fury. "I said, *get out!*"

He held up both hands. "Okay, okay." He exhaled dramatically and backed away, still holding his palms out toward her, as if warding off a crazy person.

His patronizing body language strengthened her wrath. She stood and glared at him. A million words batted around inside her head, trying to form into phrases that would make sense. "How could you?" she finally managed.

He'd reached the door. "How could I?" He furrowed his brow. "How could I what?"

What could she say to that? No way could he *not* know about her new song. She's played it so many times, and with such volume, everyone in the office had heard it.

She pointed at the door with a trembling hand and started to tell him again to leave, but he, looking genuinely bewildered, left before she had a chance. She shut the door behind him, and though she didn't mean to, she slammed it so hard that the whole wall shook. This embarrassed her. She wasn't a child, and didn't want to be acting like one, so she forced herself to take several long breaths, but this proved harder than she'd expected. Each breath grew shorter and shorter until she felt like she couldn't get enough air, and this caused a panicky feeling that made her breathe even faster. Was she hyperventilating? She didn't know. She'd never hyperventilated before. She sat down on her couch and closed her eyes and tried to reason with herself. *It's just one song. It's not the end of the world. Maggie can still record it in a few years, once the hype from Branch's song dies down, or even sooner if he doesn't release the song as a single.*

All this was true, and she knew it was, but this reasoning did little to comfort her heart. She was angry, sure, and she believed she had every reason to be, but another emotion was battling anger for first place. At first, she couldn't identify it, but after some thought, and some more deep breathing, she thought maybe she was just hurt that Logan had done such a thing to her. She knew that Chloe doing the same thing wouldn't have had nearly the same effect. But it hadn't been Chloe, or any other competitive Nashville songwriter. It had been Logan. Why this bothered her so much, she had no idea. Maybe because *he's* the one who reintroduced her to that ridiculous cliché phrase. He's the one who'd given her the song idea, and then basically gone and written his own version.

Like an arrow from an unseen archer, a new thought pierced her mind. What if he'd written his song first? Would she have known about it? Logan wrote a lot of songs. No way had she heard them all. Her anger rushed out of her, replaced by a wave of nausea. He could've written the song *years* ago, and if that was the case, she had sure just made an idiot of herself. What must Logan be thinking? She was so embarrassed, she wanted the couch to absorb her. She wanted to sink into its cushions and become part of it for the rest of her life. It wouldn't be so bad, being a couch.

A new voice in her head piped up: *Don't feel too bad until you find out who wrote their song first.* Alone in her office, she nodded in agreement with this voice. She was starting to feel a little goofy. She didn't usually have so many voices in her head.

She stood up, smoothed her hair away from her face, and took some shaky steps toward her door. Her chest still hurt, but at least she was breathing now. She gingerly opened the door and peeked out into the hallway: nobody in sight. Thank the heavens. She tiptoed down the hall toward Suzette's office and just as she was about to raise her hand to knock on the door, it opened to reveal Logan ready to exit. They locked eyes, and again her brain scrambled for something to say. It was too soon to apologize—not until she'd learned whether or not he'd stolen her idea. So she tried to keep her face impassive, even though his looked a little sad, and he brushed by her without a word.

Suzette sat at her desk. "Come on in. I was just about to buzz you."

Feeling as though she'd been called to the principal's office, Hannah entered the room and sat down. She left the door open, as it usually was. It was weird that it had been shut during Logan's visit.

"You want to tell me what's going on?" She looked more annoyed than concerned.

Hannah took a deep breath. "Do you know when Logan wrote this song that Branch is going to record?"

Suzette scowled. "What does that have to do with anything?"

Hannah held up a hand. "It matters, I promise. I'll explain. Just ... please ... can you tell me, did he write it recently, as in the last few days?"

Suzette's scowl deepened. "Hannah, I know you are an incredibly ambitious artist, and I admire that about you, but ..." She paused and softened her expression. "Well, right now, honey, that ambition isn't looking too good on you."

What? What had Logan said to her? "I'm not *jealous* of Logan Hawkins! Are you kidding me?" She knew she sounded shrieky and tried to rein it in. "I know this song is a big deal, Suzette, and I don't begrudge him his success. It's just the *content* of the song I'm taking issue with. Surely you've noticed some resemblance?"

There was a long pause as Suzette examined her. "Resemblance to what?"

Was she serious? "Resemblance to my new song," Hannah said slowly.

Another long pause. Suzette leaned back in her chair and continued to study Hannah as if she was about to do something really interesting and Suzette didn't want to miss it. "The song you sent to Maggie Hammer?"

Finally, they were getting somewhere. "Yes. That song. Do you know if Logan wrote his song before I wrote that one?" She was suddenly self-conscious about how petty she sounded. "Look, if he wrote the song in the last week, then I can live with it. I'm not going to do anything crazy. But if he wrote it years ago, then I need to know that, because then I have no reason to be angry with him." *And I have reason to apologize to him*, she silently added.

Suzette shook her head slowly. "I'm still not following."

Hannah took a long, shaky breath. How was this so complicated? "I just want to know if he stole my idea, that's all. If he did, I'll manage, but if he didn't, I'd like to know that."

Suzette raised an eyebrow. "*Stole* your idea? Why, is your Maggie Hammer song about stopping and smelling the roses?"

It was Hannah's turn to be stymied. How could she not know that? "Of course it is." She forced a fake laugh, sub-consciously trying to ease the tension in the room. "I know you listen to a lot of songs, but surely you haven't forgotten already."

Suzette ran a hand over the blotter on her desk. Her eyes followed her fingers as she did this. "Hannah," she said slowly, without looking up, "I have never heard your Maggie Hammer song."

"Of course you have!" Hannah said quickly. "These walls aren't that thick!"

Suzette gave her a small smile that looked a little sad. "Sure, I remember hearing the keyboard, but I had no idea what the song was about. I've never heard a single lyric." She paused. "Did Maggie say she wanted to cut it?"

Hannah was still processing the bit about the keyboard drowning out her voice. That meant that Logan hadn't heard the lyrics either, didn't it? Suzette was staring at her expectantly, and Hannah realized she was waiting for an answer. "Oh, uh, no, I haven't heard back from her yet."

Suzette nodded somberly. "She's probably not going to want to cut it now, but not all is lost. Tuck it away, and we'll start shopping it around in a year or so."

Suzette wasn't getting it. Hannah wasn't upset about that part of it—at least, not very. She was more upset about the idea of Logan betraying her, but as she thought about how to explain this to her boss, she realized how ridiculous she sounded. Logan and she weren't even friends. How could she expect some kind of loyalty? He'd been the one to mention the phrase, and he'd gone and written a song about it. She was upset, but she didn't really have any right to be. She had to eat crow.

She stood up. "You know what? Never mind. I'm sorry I got so upset." Her voice started to tremble, and she turned to go before the waterworks started, still dying to know *when* Logan had penned his roses song.

Chapter 18

Logan sat in his office staring down at Otis. His elation had been nearly banished by Hannah's bizarre reaction to his news. What was wrong with her? And more importantly, why was her weirdness affecting him so much? He wanted to go talk to her. He was sure that if they could have a conversation, they could figure things out. But Hannah had made it clear that she didn't want to talk to him. Was she the moodiest woman on the planet, or did he just have a really bad effect on her? His grandmother had always told him that some people just didn't mix, like oil and water. Maybe Hannah and he were like that. This thought made him sad.

He decided to take Otis out for some fresh air, mostly because he needed some himself. He scooped the dog up into his arms. Though Otis was perfectly capable of exiting the building on his own four legs, Logan wanted the closeness of carrying him.

Out in the bright sunshine of Platinum Publishing's backyard, he put Otis down in the grass.

Otis promptly peed. It was a good thing Logan had decided to go outside when he did. When he'd finished, Otis looked up at him with wide eyes, as if waiting for praise for doing his business.

Logan supplied this praise and then sat on the picnic table's bench with his back to the table. He put his elbows on the table's top and then leaned back and turned his face up to the sky. He closed his eyes and enjoyed the feeling of sunlight on his face. It felt heavenly. *Maybe I should try writing some songs out here*, he thought and then remembered his neighbors. A lot of people lived in that house. Maybe he didn't want them all listening to his works in progress. And then, as if his thoughts had summoned her, Willow was climbing over the fence.

"Howdy, stranger," she said playfully as she sashayed his way.

She was cute, but he knew she didn't use the word howdy when talking to most people, and this annoyed him. What about him had made her think she should use the word *howdy* to greet him?

"Hi."

She sat beside him, close enough to brush against his arm. "May I join you?"

He pulled his arms off the table and leaned forward. "Sure. Why not?"

She smelled like incense.

He sneezed. "Excuse me," he said, pinching his nose and sounding a bit like Charlie Brown's teacher.

She did not bless him.

This annoyed him.

"Are you allergic to Otis?"

What? Was she joking? He studied her face to see if she was kidding. He couldn't tell. She reached to pat Otis's head, but he scooted away from her touch. Logan couldn't blame him, considering how strong that incense must be to his little nose.

"Why so glum?" Willow asked, still looking at Otis, so Logan didn't know which of them she was asking.

When she didn't clarify, Logan answered, "Not glum. Just tired, I guess."

"I bet. So, what's the scoop on Otis? How's he doing?"

Logan wasn't in the mood for chitchat, but he was touched that she'd asked for details. "He's good, actually. He's tolerating the new cancer meds really well, and he hasn't had a seizure in days. His doc is very hopeful." Logan smiled. It felt good to say these positive things aloud, made them feel truer somehow. "I just can't wait for him to start acting like himself again." Logan hated to see him lethargic, hated not knowing whether Otis was only tired or whether he was in pain. Not for the first time, he wished dogs could talk.

He was staring down at his faithful pal when he realized Willow's face was awfully close to his own. He looked up to see what was happening, but before he could figure it out and respond accordingly, Willow's lips were on his. He jerked away a little, mostly from the shock of it, but she pressed in. Her lips were full and warm and sweet, and once he'd gotten over the surprise, he found the kiss wasn't so bad. She ran a hand along his cheek, and he felt comforted.

She pulled away.

He felt self-conscious. "What was that for?"

She shrugged coyly. "I just thought you needed it."

Maybe he did? He smiled at her. Then he saw Hannah watching him through the back door's screen window, and he was overcome with guilt. When their eyes met, she disappeared back into the shadows of indoors.

"You okay?" Willow asked. She hadn't seen Hannah, or at least was doing a good job of pretending she hadn't seen her.

"Yeah, I'm fine." This was a lie. The guilt was making him ill. He didn't understand this. He and Hannah didn't have anything going romantically. They weren't even friends. In fact, right now, she apparently hated him and he didn't even know why. So why was he feeling so bad about her catching him kissing someone?

Chapter 19

Hannah knew she was behaving unstably and was desperate to get a grip. But she didn't think this was going to happen at Platinum. She needed to get out of there for a bit. She was beyond embarrassed by her behavior and couldn't bear to face any of these people. She grabbed her purse and keys and speed walked for her car. She would've run, but she didn't want people to see her looking even crazier. In her hurry to unlock her car door, she dropped her keys. She looked around to see if anyone had seen this, but no one appeared to be following her out of Platinum. She felt silly. Who did she think was going to follow her out? Suzette? Logan? Why would they? Suzette probably thought she was some overly emotional artist having a nervous breakdown from all the jealousy. She probably didn't want to be anywhere near Hannah. And Logan was obviously busy in the backyard. She finally got the keys to work and was soon backing out onto the street, almost nicking one of the giant rubber garbage cans at the end of the driveway as she cut the wheel. She breathed a relieved prayer that she hadn't added trash vandalism to her long list of offenses for the day.

She knew she shouldn't be driving when she was so upset, and vowed to get off the road soon. She didn't want to go all the way home, and looked for a close spot. Immediately, she saw an open space right in front of a small bar she'd never been to. Perfect. Wasn't a small bar where every country songwriter went to process their emotions?

She took a deep breath to steady herself and climbed out of the car. On her way in, she looked furtively over each shoulder, and then felt foolish. *No one cares what you're doing*, Hannah told herself, and even if they did, there's nothing wrong with going to a bar. Besides, it was almost five o'clock.

She was grateful that the interior was dimly lit and chose a table in the corner. A petite server wearing a lot of makeup and chewing a wad of gum the size of a golf ball approached her with a menu. "Would you like something to drink?"

Hannah wasn't much of a drinker, but she'd chosen this particular location for her mental health break, and now she felt pressure to fit in. "Sure, thanks, can I get a glass of wine?"

The server looked annoyed. "Any particular kind?"

Hannah had no idea. She'd only had wine a handful of times, and someone else had always picked it out. "Something sweet?"

Further annoyed and without a word, the server spun on her heel to go select Hannah's beverage. Hannah looked around the room then and saw that she wasn't exactly in a wine kind of place. There was a man at the bar, staring into his glass as if trying to read tea leaves. Another man sat in the corner, looking up at a quiet television. The third patron sat alone in a booth on the other side of the room staring at her. Hannah quickly dropped her eyes. It didn't matter, she told herself. This was as good a place to collect her thoughts as any. She tipped her head back and closed her eyes, trying to be rational. The truth was that Logan probably hadn't stolen anything, and even if he had known about her version of the song, she had no claim to that clichéd phrase. He could use it if he wanted to, no matter what she'd been doing with it the past several days. He'd done well with it. His popularity was about to blow up, and she was truly happy for him. So, her sense of betrayal had been completely imaginary. She didn't know if she'd ever felt so foolish. She had to apologize to him. And she had to apologize to Suzette. She wished she could explain herself to her boss, but she didn't think Suzette would understand. Hannah barely understood herself. She'd put so much hope into that stupid song. She'd gotten too excited about it. A rookie mistake, putting all your hypothetical eggs into one hypothetical basket that no one else had even heard yet.

But this wasn't *all* about the song, was it? Why was she so emotional around Logan? She was normally an emotionally healthy woman. Why did he make her experience a wide range of ridiculous feelings? From annoyance to frustration to anger to jealousy? She allowed herself to ask the question she didn't want to ask: Was she attracted to Logan? It didn't seem possible. Of course, he was very good-looking, but he was like a little boy trapped in a grown-up cowboy body. And while Hannah was well aware that opposites do attract, Logan and she weren't opposites. They had a lot in common, more than most people, even. But he was childish, and she was a professional. They weren't even friends—more like enemies most of the time.

Wearing no expression at all, the server set a glass of pink wine in front of her. "Would you like something to eat?"

"Oh, I'm sorry." Hannah tried to flip open the menu, but it wouldn't open. "I haven't even looked at the menu yet."

"It's only one page."

Feeling foolish, she saw that yes, the menu couldn't be opened because it was only one page. She flipped it over. It wasn't even front and back. It was literally one page.

"I'm in no hurry. Here till closing." The woman gave her a tired smile. "So, you can take your time looking at the many options or I can just tell you that it's basically burgers, fries, and onion rings."

Hannah chuckled. "Okay, then, what do you recommend?"

"The bacon burger is pretty good. It comes with barbecue sauce."

With an excessively dramatic flair, Hannah mimed closing the unopenable menu and then handed it over. "That sounds wonderful. Thanks." Hannah watched her walk away, wondering how well a barbecue sauce bacon burger would go with wine. How that would probably make all the Nashville foodies cringe. Oh well, no one needed to know. She took a sip of the chilled wine and smacked her lips at the tartness of it. It was good, yummier than she'd expected, and she took another drink. A new warmth flowed through her, and she felt her body, as well as her emotions, relax. She realized how foreign that feeling was to her—relaxation. No wonder people liked wine.

The bar's front door opened and Logan Hawkins stepped inside. Hannah's relaxed feeling vanished.

Chapter 20

Logan stood frozen in the doorway. It was so dark inside the bar that it was difficult to see anything. But even once he'd located Hannah, sitting alone in the corner, his feet still refused to move. What was he thinking, coming in here, when he had people back at the office waiting for cake? He reminded himself how upset he'd been when he saw Hannah driving away from Platinum, and how worried he was that he had done something to upset her. He wasn't the type to let things build up. Even if Hannah hated him, even if he'd done something terrible he didn't know about, he wanted to get it out in the open. Even if it couldn't be fixed, he didn't want to keep it buried like a painful mystery.

Hannah took a drink from a wine glass that looked almost empty, and this sight was so unexpected that Logan laughed out loud. He had never taken Hannah for much of a drinker. He didn't think she'd ever take the time. Of course, he didn't know why she hated him, and he had never expected to find her in a place like this either, so there was apparently a lot he didn't know about Hannah Carter.

He finally got his legs to move and slowly approached her table. He half-expected her to bark at him and send him on his way again, but the expression on her face was soft, so he picked up his pace. "May I join you?"

She motioned toward the chair opposite her. "Please."

He took his hat off and set it on the windowsill beside the table, then folded his arms and put them on the table. The moment felt awkward, and he was tempted to make some quip, say something funny to break the tension, but he stopped himself. He knew that whatever was going on with Hannah was serious, and figured she wouldn't appreciate an attempt at levity.

Finally, as the uncomfortable silence stretched out between them, they both started talking at the same time. Their words collided in the jumble between them, and both of them stopped talking to laugh. He felt the tension melt away, and his chest relaxed in relief. "Please, you go first."

She looked nervous. He couldn't remember her ever looking nervous. She was always so confident. He wanted to say something encouraging, something to bolster her to say what she needed to say, but he'd told her that she could speak first, and he didn't want to interrupt her again.

She opened her mouth, and still nothing came out.

He tried to hide his impatience, tried to *be* patient. He could tell that, whatever this was, it was hard for her.

"Hey, stranger!" Mary Jo interrupted their discomfort.

"Hey, Mary Jo! I didn't know you worked here now!"

She gave his shoulder a friendly squeeze, and he wished that she hadn't. "Um, yeah, Ricky fired me a few months ago."

"Oh yeah? Sorry to hear that. I hear he can be tough to work for."

"He sure is. You still hang out there?"

Now that he knew she'd been fired from The Blue Umbrella, he didn't want to admit he still went there. "Not as much as I used to. That woman I was always with, she really liked that place, but we broke up."

Mary Jo glanced at Hannah. "Well, that's too bad, but it looks like you're doing all right for yourself now."

Logan started to correct her, started to tell her that he and Hannah just worked together, that they were barely even friends, but he stopped himself. What was the harm in letting her think that Hannah was his girlfriend? He would be proud to have a girlfriend as smart and beautiful as her.

"So, a Coke, no ice?"

He smiled, touched that she remembered. It had been a while. He tapped his temple with one finger. "Steel trap you got there."

She laughed. "Hardly. You want anything to eat?"

He looked at Hannah. He didn't want to presume. Did she want to stick around long enough to eat something? "No, thank you. Just the Coke." He could stand to eat, but he could also wait, in case Hannah was in a hurry to get rid of him.

"No, please order something," Hannah said. "I've got food coming soon and I'll feel super awkward eating if you're not eating. And it's my treat. Just don't order the lobster." Hannah laughed as if that was the funniest thing she'd ever heard, and Mary Jo joined in.

Well, look at that. Hannah Carter being funny. "Okay, then, I guess I'll have what she's having." He hoped she hadn't ordered a salad.

Mary Jo vanished into the shadows.

"She sure is in a better mood since you showed up."

His cheeks grew warm and he looked down at his hands. "Nah, she's just flirting her way to a good tip. So ..." He forced himself to look her in the eyes even though it unnerved him to do so. "I think you were about to say something?"

She took a big breath. "Definitely." She drained the last of her glass of wine and then quickly said, "I owe you a gargantuan apology."

Chapter 21

The wine was providing Hannah with a little extra courage, but not enough. "I need to ask you something ... so that I can know how to explain myself best."

Logan looked scared.

Even under the circumstances, she found his fear amusing. It made her feel a little powerful to be able to scare him. "Did you know that I recently wrote a song called 'No Time for Roses'?"

Understanding fell over his face like a curtain, and he leaned back in his chair. "Oh no."

This was already going better than she could've imagined. He was reading her mind. She could tell he felt horrible, and she hadn't even finished her explanation. "I'll take that as a no."

"I didn't know. I'm so sorry."

She held up a hand to stall his apology. "No, really, I'm the one who's sorry. I played it over and over so loudly that I thought everybody in the house had heard it a hundred times, and then, like a fool, when I heard the title of your new song, I thought you'd stolen my idea." She was certain she'd never felt so childish.

He opened his mouth, but she didn't let him interrupt. "I know that's ridiculous. Stop and smell the roses is an ancient idea, and you're the one who brought it up when we were talking, so you *can't* steal it. And for all I know, you wrote that song years ago, so I'm really sorry. My mind jumped to the worst case scenario, and I felt betrayed, which is so, so stupid." With her elbows on the table, she put her head in her hands and mumbled, "I am so embarrassed." She wanted more wine.

He reached out and rubbed one knuckle against her forearm, which sent unexpected tingles up her arm. He slowly pulled his hand away and she wished he hadn't. She peeked out through her fingers at him, and couldn't believe the compassion in his eyes. She'd provided him with the perfect opportunity to poke fun at her for being a mental mushroom, and here he was caring about her feelings. Maybe he could be serious once in a while.

"I'm so sorry. No, I just wrote the song a few days ago, and it *was* inspired by our conversation, but I had no idea that you were working on a song about the same thing." He furrowed his brow and gave her a smile. "Though it sounds like your take on it might be a little different?"

She smiled and swatted at a single tear of relief that was sneaking down her cheek. "Yeah, just a little. I bet yours is about lying in the back of a pickup truck staring up at the sky, chewing on a single piece of hay, doing absolutely nothing."

He tipped his head back and laughed, a sound she found incredibly rewarding. "Yeah, you're close. And I bet yours is about working around the clock and not taking any breaks because we're all going to die soon."

She burst out with laughter as Mary Jo slid a giant burger in front of her. She hadn't even been hungry, but the combination of getting all of this off her chest and the sight and smell of that burger made her ravenous. Mary Jo offered her another glass of wine, and she declined. She picked up the saltshaker and then looked at Logan. "This isn't sugar, right?"

He laughed. "Not that I know of. I've never been here before, but I can't promise someone else hasn't made a swap."

Knowing she was smiling foolishly, she salted her fries, squirted some ketchup onto the edge of her plate, and then stopped fiddling and looked at him.

"What?"

"Nothing. I'm just waiting for you to get your burger."

"Oh, no, go ahead. Don't wait for me. I couldn't live with myself if I denied you of that monstrous chunk of beef while it's still hot."

He was right about the burger's monstrosity, and no way was she going to try to take a bite out of it with him staring at her. She was certain that barbecue sauce would squirt out in multiple directions, including directly at him, and probably drip down her chin as well. She wanted him to be distracted by his own sloppy meal when that happened.

"Maybe we should have some sort of contest," he said. "We could each sing our song and then ask people to vote on whose philosophy is more persuasive."

She laughed. "No, thank you. I'm just going to tuck the song away for a while. I've already sent it to Maggie Hammer, but I'm sure she won't record it once she learns what Branch is doing."

Mary Jo returned and slid another burger in front of Logan. He thanked her with more charm than any man should be allowed to possess. She realized she was staring at him and stopped herself, but it was too late.

"What? Do I have something stuck between my teeth?"

She laughed and shook her head. "No, I just can't believe you followed me here." As soon it she'd said the words, she wished she hadn't. It was true that she was surprised he had followed her, and she didn't know what it meant, but she didn't need to call him out for it and put him on the spot like that.

He didn't seem rattled, though. "I didn't follow you here, at least, not on purpose. Suzie Q sent me to fetch my own cake, and I saw your car parked out front and thought you'd lost your mind. Thought maybe I should check on you, make sure you're okay."

Now she was even more embarrassed. She'd accused him of caring enough to follow her, and he'd done nothing of the sort.

"Although, I must admit that it bothered me a whole heap having you be that mad at me. So if I had known that you were leaving to sneak off to some dangerous dive bar in the middle of the day, I might just have followed you." He shoved some fries into his smiling mouth.

"It's not the middle of the day," she protested. "It's almost five o'clock." She leaned toward him and lowered her voice. "You really think this place is dangerous?"

He chuckled. "I wouldn't hang out here."

This made her oddly proud of herself.

"There's one more thing I want to talk to you about," he said, "and I just want to throw it out there." He swallowed. "I want you to know something, so I'm going to tell you, but it doesn't have to mean anything."

What on earth was he about to say? She held her breath.

"What you saw in the backyard was nothing. She kissed me, it's true, but there's nothing going on between Willow and me."

She nodded and then quickly looked down at her burger. Why was he telling her this? Did he think she cared that he was kissing someone? Why would she care about that? But, it was true that she did care. So, how did he know that? Or did he even know it? Was he just suspicious? And if he was, was this a good thing? She didn't even know how she felt about him. Did she like him? And if she did, did she want him to know that?

Chapter 22

Maybe I shouldn't have said that last part, Logan thought, as now Hannah seemed unreasonably enthralled with her burger. She wouldn't even look at him and her leg was bouncing up and down as if she was getting ready to bolt out of the bar any second. His phone buzzed in his pocket, and he yanked it out, scared it was Chloe calling about Otis.

It was. He was having another seizure, and she didn't know what to do.

He looked at Hannah. "I'm so sorry. I have to go."

Her eyes finally met his, and they were wide with concern. "Is it Otis?"

He nodded, his throat tight. He got up, pulling his wallet out of the back pocket of his jeans.

"I'll come with you." She started to stand.

"No, no, you stay and finish your burger." He threw two twenties on the table, then hesitated because he had no idea how much those burgers were. No, that had to be enough. They weren't at The Ritz. He stuffed his wallet back into his pocket.

She hesitated, half-standing. "Do you want me to wait and have your meal boxed up? I could bring it to you."

He had less than no appetite. "No, that's okay."

She straightened up and glanced down at his money. "I doubt your burger cost forty dollars."

"My treat."

She grabbed her purse and headed for the door. "I'll meet you back at Platinum."

This was ridiculous. She didn't need to leave, and she hadn't touched her food. He studied her for a second, wondering how much wine she'd had before he'd gotten there. "Are you okay to drive?"

She stared at the table, as if the answer to that lie there. "I don't know." Her eyes drifted to his. "Am I? I only had one glass of wine."

He chuckled. "I have no idea. But just to be safe, you should either stay and eat your food"—he opened the door for her—"or ride with me."

She quickly ducked under his arm and out onto the sidewalk. "Thanks."

Suddenly feeling self-conscious, he led her to his truck and opened the door for her. She climbed up into the Ford as if she'd done it a thousand times before, and as she sat, a cloud of Otis hair shot up into the air and engulfed her. Logan's face got hot. "Sorry, that's usually Otis's seat."

"No worries." She flashed him a beautiful smile, and amazingly, *didn't* sneeze.

He shut the door and hurried around to his side.

"What's going on?" she asked as he started the engine.

"Not sure. Chloe says he had another seizure. They've messed with his epilepsy meds a bunch since they found the cancer, and so I never really know when these seizures are going to happen."

"Are they dangerous?" She sounded choked up.

The sound of the emotion in her voice made his eyes fill with water. He looked out his side window to hide his tears from her. "They can be, especially if they happen often, or if they last too long." With difficulty, he swallowed. "He was a rescue, so who knows what happened to him early in life. But when I adopted him, they told me he had aggression, but he doesn't, not really. After a dog has a seizure, they can get really confused and sometimes aggressive. I'm betting that's what happened. Though, it's never happened with me."

"He probably knows he's safe with you. So when he comes around, he might be confused, but he's comforted by your presence."

His heart warmed at her words. "Maybe. And I've had him on anticonvulsant meds since the beginning, so there haven't been very many seizures." He let out a long breath. "Until now."

"Right. But this is only a season. It won't last long. Otis is going to come through this and be good as new."

He nodded, not trusting himself to speak.

They rode the rest of the way to the office in silence, and then walked wordlessly, side by side, up the walkway to the front door, which he opened for her.

Suzie Q met them there, her face lined with worry. "I'm so sorry, Logan."

Her reaction seemed excessive. How bad had the seizure been? Forgetting about Hannah for the moment, he rushed down the hallway to his office.

Otis lay on his side, his head tipped back and his eyes closed. He was still. Chloe sat on the floor beside him, with tears running down her cheeks. Whatever semblance of control he'd had over his emotions left him then as he slowly approached his best friend's lifeless body. He knelt beside him and placed his hand on Otis's chest.

A loud bark of a laugh burst out of Logan, and Chloe jumped. "He's breathing!" Logan cried. His hand rose and fell on Otis's small chest. Logan laughed again. "He's breathing," he said, more quietly. He'd never felt such sweet relief in his life.

Hannah placed a gentle hand on his shoulder, and he thought his heart might burst with joy.

"Sorry, Logan," Chloe said quietly. "I didn't mean to make you think he had left us. I was just scared because he's not waking up."

This could hardly qualify as bad news, Logan thought. Not compared to what he'd previously thought. "And you're sure he had a seizure."

"I'm sure. It was awful. I didn't know what to do. I felt so helpless."

"I don't think it causes him any pain," Logan tried to comfort her. "Bothers us more than him. Still, I should probably get him to the vet if he's not waking up." He slid his hands under Otis's warm body. Was he too warm?

"Want some company?" Hannah asked. Her hand slid off his shoulder as he came to his feet.

"Sure, thank you. Would you get the doors for me?"

Hannah hurried to his office door, which still stood open. Then she practically ran to the front door, which Suzie Q opened before Hannah could get there.

"Well, I'll at least get the truck door." She ran toward his side of the truck.

"Hang on. The keys are in my pocket." Well, this was awkward. He could probably hold Otis with one arm so he could get the keys out himself, but not without half of Otis's body flopping around, and he wanted to be gentle with the dog. He glanced down at his pocket, feeling sheepish. "Would you mind?"

Chapter 23

Well, *this is awkward. There are probably a lot of women who would be thrilled to reach into the pocket of Logan Hawkins's tight blue jeans.* But was she one of them? She wasn't sure. Tentatively, as though she were trying to grab a venomous snake by the neck, she reached out toward Logan's hip.

Then she came to her senses. Her coworker—her, dare she say it, *friend*—was standing there waiting, patiently holding his probably-dying dog. And he needed this itty-bitty favor from her. And she was taking forever, turning it into this big thing. She needed to get a grip. She stepped behind him to make the angle more natural, so that she could slide her hand into his pocket as if it were her own. The angle was still a little off, because he was so much taller than her, but her fingertips quickly found the key ring, and she pulled the keys out. Feeling as though she'd just taken first in a difficult obstacle course, she started to hand the keys to him and then realized that his hands were just as full as they'd been ten seconds ago. She then fumbled with the keys to locate the unlock button on the fob, which she pushed. The locks clicked open. "There." She ripped the truck door open. "Sorry it took me so long."

He frowned and laughed at the same time, a combination only he could pull off. "It took you like five seconds." He climbed into his truck, settling most of Otis on his lap, but he kept his left arm under Otis's neck. He reached his right hand out to her, and for a second, she didn't know why, but then she realized he still needed his keys.

She handed them to him and then started to run around the truck so she could jump in. She wanted to go with him, and was afraid he'd leave her. When she reached the front grill, she realized his door still stood open, and she hurried back to shut it. *I must look like a headless hen.* She hoped Logan had enough on his mind that he wasn't paying any attention to her panicked antics.

They finally got underway and Logan glanced down at his dog every three seconds.

"I'm sorry. I should've offered to drive." Why hadn't she thought of that?

"That's okay. I didn't think of it, and besides, you still haven't eaten anything."

"Oh for Pete's sake, it was one glass of wine, and I don't feel anything anymore." She realized he was smirking. Was he just messing with her? At a time like this? "Where is the animal hospital?"

"Fryeburg Street."

"Where is that?"

"Not far." He sounded distant, distracted.

Should she leave him alone with his thoughts or try to distract him from them?

She opted for the latter. "You do realize, Otis is going to get better and then you're going to write a smash hit about all this. It will be 'Feed Jake' all over again."

He smiled. "Then he'd better get better, because I don't write sad songs."

Maybe it was time he did. Wasn't it healthy to write about all emotions, even the hard ones?

"And for the record, I'd rather write another 'Old Red.'"

Her chest filled with warmth at the thought of that beautiful song. "You're right. That treasure is timeless. A real love song. And I don't even like love songs."

"Finally, we agree on something."

Wait. What had they agreed on? That the song was a timeless treasure or that they didn't like love songs? It must have been the first, because the man wrote love songs. Of course, that didn't mean he liked or believed in what he was writing. He'd made it clear that he was comfortable writing hogwash lyrics.

He read her mind. "I meant that we agree on 'Old Red' being the perfect love song, not that I don't believe in love songs."

"I figured," she lied.

After a pause, he asked, "You seriously don't write love songs?"

Was this really the time to discuss this? Maybe it was. She had wanted to distract him. "That is correct. There are enough love songs in the world."

He guffawed. "Obviously not, 'cause people keep buying the new ones."

Did this guy base all his artistic theories on what would sell? She rolled her eyes. "Fair enough." She didn't want to argue with him.

"Why?"

"Why what?"

"Why don't you believe in love songs?"

Had she said that? Hadn't she only said that there were already enough of them in the world?

He didn't let her answer. "I mean, I get that most of them are cheesy." He let go of the wheel long enough to turn his blinker on and then stopped the truck to wait for an opening in traffic. "But love is kind of cheesy, so when you're in love, you're in the mood for cheesy. Haven't you ever been in love, Hannah?" His voice sounded playful.

Why was he teasing her about her love life when his dog lay dying in his arms? Or was he teasing her about her love life *because* his dog lay dying in his arms? She didn't want to answer him. He was obviously expecting her too. "Yes," she said, grudgingly. "I've been in love. Hasn't everyone?"

There was a long pause. "And?"

"And what?"

"That's all you're going to say?" A hole opened up in the traffic, and he pulled onto a side street.

She looked up at the sign. Fryeburg Street. They were almost there. Thank God. "I'm not sure what else you want me to say."

"I want you to tell me why you don't believe in love songs."

"Because I don't believe in love."

He barked out a laugh. "How's that possible?"

She was growing frustrated. Why was he prying so? "I don't know. Because it's just never worked out for me."

"Fine. Sorry to be nosy." Now he sounded injured.

She blew out a puff of air. Fine. She would engage. If this is what Logan needed from her in his time of crisis, she would oblige. "I used to be kind of boy crazy. Had lots of crushes. Met a few who I thought were 'the one.'" She cringed at her own foolishness.

"And?"

Man, he was insatiable. "And none of them liked me back. Simple as that."

His head snapped toward her and he stared at her as though he were studying her.

"Please watch the road."

He snickered and turned his eyes front. "I find that hard to believe."

"Yeah. I did too. I mean, I'm not a super model or anything. But I'm not that bad. But still, no one has ever been interested, so I just sort of gave up. Or rather, the desire for love wore off. And I'm happier now, honestly. I'm not just saying that. I'd rather just focus on me, on my life, on doing what I love and what I'm good at, than constantly trying to make people like me and getting rejected over and over. That game got old."

Logan was pulling into the parking lot of the animal hospital before she'd even realized they were there. He parked the truck, turned off the engine, and leveled a gaze at her. His eyes were firm, sincere, and his gaze took her breath away. "You're absolutely beautiful, Hannah."

She gazed back, speechless, not moving, not breathing. What? How was she supposed to respond to that?

THE SONGWRITER'S RIVAL

"Now, would your beautiful self please come open my truck door?"

Chapter 24

Logan and Hannah sat shoulder to shoulder in the crowded waiting room, on a padded bench that wasn't padded enough. Otis was still in his arms. Still breathing, but still very much unconscious. He was trying not to think about what that might mean. He wasn't ready to lose this dog, and would do almost anything to avoid that.

A woman in scrubs stepped out from behind the double doors. "Otis?" She raised her eyes at Logan and smiled. "You can come on back."

Logan stood up, Otis's small body feeling unusually heavy in his arms. He looked back at Hannah, who hadn't moved. Did she not want to come? He wanted her to.

"I can wait here, if you want." She sounded like a mouse.

"Or you can come along." He forced a chuckle. "I may need the emotional support."

She sprang up then and followed him as he followed the woman in scrubs, who led him into a small exam room. "Dr. Dewitt will be right with you." She closed the door behind her, leaving the motley threesome alone.

Logan laid Otis out on the table, and he didn't stir, a sight which tightened Logan's chest with fear. Was this really it? Had they come this far fighting cancer just to die of a preventable seizure? He stroked Otis's soft head. Surely, this couldn't be it.

The door opened and Dr. Dewitt breezed in. "Sorry to keep you waiting. What's going on?"

Logan explained the situation as best he could. The vet nodded his understanding as he began to examine Otis. As Logan talked, he became aware of Hannah's presence beside him. Her closeness brought him reassurance and comfort. How could having someone so uptight nearby give him peace? He didn't know.

Dr. Dewitt pulled the stethoscope out of his ears. "Okay, this is rare, but it can happen after seizures." He sighed. "What I'd like to do is give him some fluids, some oxygen, and some time. His vitals are good, and I think he'll come out of it on his own."

There was a pause. "And if he doesn't?" Logan didn't want to think it, but there it was.

Hannah slid her hand over his, which was holding onto the table with white knuckles.

"He will."

Was the doctor that confident? Or was he faking it for Logan's sake? "He just needs some R&R." He ran a hand down Otis's back. "I've got a kennel with his name on it. We'll make him very comfortable."

Logan laughed. "Do you have one for me? I could use some R&R too."

Hannah flinched beside him, but he didn't know why.

"I do have a kennel you'd fit in, but then you wouldn't be able to see Otis. So, is that how you want to proceed? I can move him there right now."

Logan nodded and swallowed hard. "Whatever you think is best."

The kind veterinarian scooped Otis up and carried him out. "Elise will be back in a second to talk to you," he said as he was leaving. "I'll get Otis set up."

The original woman in scrubs, whose name was apparently Elise, came in almost immediately. "We're going to take good care of him," she said gently. "You're welcome to go home, and we'll call you the second he wakes up. Or, if you want, you can stay here for as long as you need to."

Of course he wanted to stay. But what about Hannah? He looked down at their hands. Hers was still on top of his, having that same unexpected calming effect. Then he looked into her eyes. "I can give you a ride back to your car? Or to the office?"

"Are you staying?" she whispered.

He nodded.

"Do you want some company?"

He nodded again. Then he looked at Elise. "Should we go back to the waiting room then?"

"You can. Or you can go sit beside Otis. He'll be in a kennel, but right now there are no other dogs in the room, so you can sit there if you want. We just need to keep the room quiet. If we get other dogs in, we might need to move you, but for now, it's up to you."

Was Hannah seriously going to go sit beside his sick dog with him? He tried to ask that question with his eyes.

"Sure. Let's go sit with Otis. I think it would be good for him to know you're close to him."

Chapter 25

Hannah didn't know why she was so invested in this sad situation, but she was. She could practically hear Logan's heart breaking, and hers was on the verge of breaking along with it. She wasn't as confident in Otis's imminent recovery as the vet was, and she didn't want Logan to be alone when the unthinkable happened.

If it happened, she corrected her thoughts. She and Logan sat in rigid office chairs beside Otis's kennel. They sat at an angle so they were half-facing Otis and half-facing each other, her left knee only a foot away from his right knee. The threesome formed a silent triangle. Otis was in one of the second tier kennels, so Logan could see him from snout to tail without moving. If Otis opened his eyes, he'd be looking directly at Logan's face.

"Why did you flinch when I said I needed some R&R?" Logan whispered, keeping his eyes riveted on Otis.

She'd flinched? She hadn't meant to. "I don't know."

He dragged his eyes away from Otis to look at her. "Oh sure you do. You jumped like my mama when I say a bad word." He chuckled, and the sound reminded her of why she'd probably flinched.

"I think I was just surprised that you'd be joking around at a time like this."

"I'm always joking around," he said quietly, almost as if talking to himself.

"I guess that's my point," she said after a pause.

He didn't respond, and she thought the conversation was over. The silence stretched on, nothing changed, and Hannah wondered what she'd signed herself up for. How long would they wait? How long would the vet allow Logan to maintain such false hope?

"I used to be so angry," Logan said quietly, again as though engaged in a private conversation with himself.

Was he talking to her at all? Did he want her to respond? "I'm sorry?"

He chuckled. "Really. I know it's hard to believe now, but when I was seventeen, my best friend died in a dirt bike accident, and I ..." His voice trailed off and he leaned forward and put his elbows on his knees. Then he looked at the floor. "I was so mad. Like out of control rage." He paused for so long that she was certain he was done talking. Then he sat up and looked at Otis again. "I started acting out. I didn't care whether I lived or died." He chuckled again. "I think maybe I did want to die. Almost did a few times. It was like this anger was boiling inside of me every second of the day. Might sound childish now, but I still don't think it was. There's a lot to be angry about in this world. My friend didn't deserve to die. He was a good kid. No kids deserve to die. Yet they die all the time. My dad didn't deserve to lose his job. My parents didn't deserve to struggle to make ends meet." He flashed her a dazzling smile. "They don't struggle anymore." The smile slowly slid off his face. She'd never seen him look so contemplative. "War's not fair. Poverty's not fair. Hunger's not fair. Cancer's not fair." He paused again.

She didn't know what to say.

"Anyway, I was furious. I got in lots of fights, fights with people I was angry enough to kill. Thanks to the grace of God, I never managed to kill anyone, or my story would have a very different ending. Anyway, one day, I just sort of woke up. Nothing even happened that I know of to cause it. There wasn't any big pivotal event or anything. I was fishing, and was angry that I hadn't caught anything, angry that my buddy always caught more than I did, angry at him for breaking all the fishing laws, and I thought to myself, 'Self, do you want to be this angry for the rest of your life?'"

Oh no. She sensed where this was going. This was a lecture. He was trying to tell her she needed to loosen up in life. To stop and smell the roses. "Having anger issues and taking life seriously are two different things."

He looked at her again. "I never said they weren't. This isn't about you, Hannah. We're talking about me here. Do you mind?" He smirked to let her know he was kidding, but was he kidding, entirely?

She waved a hand at him. "Carry on, then."

"You asked why I made a joke when I was scared and sad, and I'm telling you. I think we're created to have faith, and I think we're supposed to rest in that faith, to give up our anger, our fear, our sadness. I made a decision that day to choose joy. Sounds kind of hokey, I know, but man, did things change. I stopped trying to drown the pain or take it out on someone else and I started trying to laugh through it instead." He tipped his head to the side and gazed at her. "And yes, this world is messed up, and there's plenty of injustice to be angry about, but this world is also hilarious."

She nodded slowly. "Okay. I guess I understand." She didn't, not really. Laugh away the world? What good would that do?

"Do you?" His intense gaze made her uncomfortable.

She squirmed in her chair and turned her eyes to Otis. "Sure."

"Great, because now we're talking about you."

"Beg your pardon?" She didn't look at him. She didn't want to talk about her. Why oh why had she opted for this particular mission?

"I admire your drive, Hannah. I admire your focus, your determination, and I'm in no way suggesting that you have anger issues. But I do wish you'd relax a little more. I wish you'd choose joy sometimes."

She rolled her shoulders back and clenched her jaw. Who was he to tell her how to live? She had joy in her life! Plenty of it!

But did she?

"Point taken," she said, just to end the conversation. "Do you think he's warm enough? It's kind of chilly in here."

Logan stood and started to unbutton his flannel.

How sweet, she thought. *He's going to give his shirt to his dog.*

But he didn't give it to his dog. Instead, he stepped behind her and draped it over her shoulders. Then he rubbed her upper arms.

Her cheeks got hot. "I didn't mean that *I* was cold."

He returned to his chair. "Do you want me to take it back?"

How was she supposed to answer that? Saying yes might offend him. "No, that's okay. Thank you. It feels nice." It did feel nice. And it smelled ambrosial.

"You're welcome." He was staring at the dog again.

Chapter 26

Logan couldn't believe that Hannah was still sitting there with Otis and him. He didn't know exactly what time they'd arrived at the animal hospital, but they'd been sitting there for quite a while. She couldn't sit still, though, so either she was feeling impatient or was physically uncomfortable—maybe both. He could tell she didn't hold out much hope. It was written all over her face. And as the sand in the hourglass drained away, so did his own optimism. How much time should he give his friend? Maybe Otis didn't want to come back. Maybe Logan should let him go. He didn't know what to do. He didn't want to give up on Otis, but he didn't want to be selfish, either. He needed to do what was best for Otis. That was his job.

Dr. Dewitt had poked his head in a few times to check on them, and he still seemed hopeful. He would tell Logan when it was time to give up, wouldn't he?

"Excuse me," Hannah said softly. "I need to find the restroom." It sounded as though she felt guilty. Guilty for leaving him. Maybe she didn't really need the bathroom. Maybe she just needed to get out of the room she was in for a minute. Either way, he couldn't blame her. But she really shouldn't have left her phone on the floor beside her chair, all exposed and unprotected, just begging him to mess with her. Without debating with his self-control, his hand shot out and snatched the phone. He was tempted to change all her contacts to Minnie Pearl, but he knew that would take her forever to undo, so, instead, he just added a few contacts of his own: Minnie Pearl, or course, as well as Beauregard the Wonder Dog (the bloodhound from Hee Haw—he was a little embarrassed to know that and thought he'd probably have to explain it to Hannah), Daisy Duke, Barney Fife, and Gomer Pyle.

He set all these phone numbers to his own, deciding this was a better prank than his original idea, because it might take her forever to notice. He hoped that, when she did notice, she would call him and ask to speak to Gomer Pyle.

He heard her footsteps and rushed to put her phone back where he'd found it. He sat up and tried to act naturally, noticing too late that he hadn't dimmed the screen. Its brightness pointed an accusing finger at him, and he was sure Hannah would notice. She gasped, and he thought he was busted, but when he looked at her, she was pointing at Otis's kennel.

Logan jumped up. "What?"

"His leg. It moved ... I think." With each word she spoke, her confidence dissipated until she sounded as though she didn't believe herself. Had she really seen something? Or had she only wanted to see something?

"Was it a mirage?" He was trying to be funny.

She didn't laugh.

He stood and reached out to lay his hand on Otis's head. Otis's eyes rolled around behind his eyelids and his tail jerked. Logan's heart jerked with it. "Holy moly! Go get the doc!" Instantly, he felt bad for barking orders at Hannah. "Please," he added in a softer tone, but she was already through the door. "Hey there, little fella," he whispered, "I'm right here."

Otis's eyelids slid up then and his tail slapped the bed. He started to push himself up, obviously excited to see Logan.

"Easy, easy, take your time." Logan continued to stroke his soft fur, glad Hannah wasn't there to see his tears.

By the time Hannah returned with Elise in tow, Otis was sitting up, wagging his tail, and trying to climb onto Logan. Logan held him in place and looked at Elise. "He wants me to grab him, but I don't want to wiggle the IV and hurt him."

"No worries." Elise reached over Logan's arms and gently freed Otis from his medical entanglements. "Sorry, Dr. Dewitt is dealing with another emergency. I'll talk to him about Otis as soon as I can, but it looks like we're in the clear. He'll want to check his vitals, but you can certainly hold him while you wait.

Logan scooped Otis up and he promptly started licking Logan's cheeks. Hannah laughed, a sweet melodic sound that made Logan's elation almost too much to bear, and ran a hand down Otis's back. Otis stopped his licking long enough to give Hannah's hand a sniff, and then returned his attention to Logan's face.

"Unreal," Hannah said softly. "You are a miracle pup."

"Yes, he is, and he has been from the beginning."

Hannah smiled up at him. "And you're a good doggie dad, Logan."

Logan had received a lot of praise from a lot of people in the last few years, but this praise from Hannah felt particularly great. "Thank you." He returned to his chair, and Hannah rolled hers closer to his. *We're like a little family*, Logan thought. This made him think of his extended family. "Would you do me a favor and text Suzie Q, let her know the good news?"

"Of course I will text *Suzette* and let her know." She reached back for her phone.

He laughed. "Why don't you just call her Suzie Q like the rest of us?" Otis finally settled down and shoved his nose into the crook of Logan's arm.

"Because her name is *Suzette*. Aren't you the one who named her Suzie Q?"

He felt proud. "Yep!"

"Well"—she finished the text and looked up at him— "I don't want to call my *boss* a baked treat."

He laughed again. "I don't call her that because of a baked treat. I call her that because of the legendary Credence Clearwater song."

She frowned. "Oh. I guess I should've assumed that, being a songwriter and all."

"Yes. You should have. But I won't tell anyone that you find baked treats more important than classic songs."

She tipped her head to the side and gave him a dirty look. It was adorable.

"So, when are we going to cowrite a song about a miracle dog?" he asked, half joking, and half hoping she'd say, *As soon as possible.*

Chapter 27

Hannah sat alone in Logan's office with Otis, who was acting as if he'd never been sick in his life. Everyone had stayed at the office late, insisting that they still needed to celebrate Logan's professional triumph. She could hear them in the front room, yukking it up, and had a feeling they were all also celebrating Otis's recovery. But Logan had thought the celebration would be too stimulating for Otis, and Hannah had quickly volunteered to sit with him. She'd opened a songwriting technique book on her phone, but she hadn't been able to focus on the words enough to comprehend anything.

She couldn't stop thinking about Logan.

She wasn't sure how it had happened, but she had developed feelings for the man. *Romantic* feelings. And now her instinct was to do whatever it took to get rid of those feelings. But did she want to? Even right now, though she could hear his voice, she still missed him. And when she was close to him, she couldn't stop looking at him. When had he gotten so handsome? And that smile that she'd used to find so irritating, she now found comforting. What was going on? She knew that intense experiences, especially those involving adrenalin, often led people to be attracted to those who had shared the experience. Was that what was going on here? It must be.

And if it wasn't?

What if she really was falling for him? Would he ... *could he* ever reciprocate those feelings? Was that even possible? He was a good-looking guy, and now, a ridiculously *successful* guy. Would he even consider her romantically, especially when she'd been so rude to him in the past?

She rubbed her eyes, physically drained and tired of spending so much time in her own head. She needed some sleep, or at least to *not* think for a while. Was that even possible for her? She loved to think, loved to analyze and problem solve, but trying to analyze and problem solve her new feelings for Logan was getting her nowhere.

"Hey there."

She jumped.

He'd sneaked up on her and now stood in the open doorway, with one arm above his head, leaning on the door jamb. He looked absolutely gorgeous. She dropped her eyes.

"You okay?" He dropped his arm and entered the room.

"Yeah, I'm okay." She tried to fake a yawn and it turned into a real one. "I'm just tired."

"No kidding. Me too. I'm totally zapped. I told them I've had enough fun. I appreciate everyone's support, but I can't keep my eyes open." He stopped talking and the silence made her uncomfortable.

Was he waiting for her to say something? Oh, maybe he was waiting for her to get out of his office. She scrambled to her feet. "Yes, I'll let you get going. Otis has been great, by the way. He seems fine."

"Good. Hey, Hannah?" He waited for her eyes to meet his before continuing. "I don't really know how to thank you for today. I don't want to be all weird and awkward, but I also don't want to let you go home without me thanking you, because it would probably be even weirder and awkwarder if I tried it tomorrow." He laughed.

Her heart tried to thump itself free of her chest. She tried to give him a calm smile. "It was nothing, really."

"No." He stepped closer to her. "It was definitely something. I was so sad and so scared, and because of you, I didn't have to do that alone." He closed the gap between them and wrapped his arms around her.

She was enveloped in his smell. She hoped with all her might that he couldn't feel how hard her heart was beating.

He let go of her abruptly, but held her at arm's length. "Are you sure you're okay?"

She nodded.

He rubbed her upper arms. "You feel ..." His voice trailed off.

"What?" What had he been about to say? She'd never been so eager to hear someone complete a sentence.

"Well, I didn't want to be critical, and I'm not. I mean, I don't *feel* critical as I say this. I'm just concerned."

What? What's wrong? Just say it!

"You just felt rigid when I hugged you. And you weren't breathing. It felt like you didn't really want me to be hugging you—"

"No," she interrupted.

"No, what?"

And now she was embarrassed again. How could she get out of this with any semblance of self-respect? "No. It wasn't that." She couldn't tell him how much she *did* want him to hug her, could she? "I don't know ... I think rigid is my default setting." She forced a laugh, and she sounded like the witch just about to bite into Gretel. "I don't know if I'm ever *not* rigid. I even have trouble with my jaw because I clench my teeth too much." Oh great, now she was oversharing. "And I do often forget to breath, you're right."

He laughed, and his laugh sounded genuine, much unlike hers. "Boy, we sure do have our work cut out for us."

Wait. Had he said *we*? What did that mean? She didn't know what it meant, and therefore, she didn't know how to respond.

"Should we try it again?"

She panicked. "Try what again?"

He smiled. "The hug?" He held up both hands. "Don't worry, I'm not coming on to you. It's just a friend-hug"—

And there it was. They were just friends. He was just being kind.

—"I just think you need a good hug right now, and frankly, so do I." He waited with arms spread for her to step into his embrace.

She wanted to have his arms around her. She was also afraid she was going to cry if she allowed that to happen. Though only hours ago, she'd had no desire for more than friendship from Logan, now it was all her heart wanted, and she felt crushed by the disappointment. She stepped around his arms and headed for the door. "That's okay. Sorry, I've got to go."

She made it halfway to the front door before the tears started falling.

This. This was why she didn't allow herself to feel things for any man. Because the rejection hurt too much. And the rejection was inevitable.

Chapter 28

Logan stared at the empty doorway that Hannah had practically run through. What had just happened? A few days ago, he would've just brushed it off as more evidence that Hannah Carter was a weirdo, but he now knew that wasn't the case. At least, she hadn't been weird with him that day. She'd been perfect.

Maybe she didn't like to be touched. He'd heard about people like that. That must be it. Shoot. He'd really crossed a line then, and he felt horribly about it. He'd be apologizing in the morning. For now, he had to get Otis home and into bed.

People reiterated their congratulations on his way out the door, and when he finally made it outside, Willow was standing on the lawn.

"Y'all are here late. Having a party?"

His instinct was to smile at the beautiful woman, but he didn't want to encourage her. "Sorry, don't mean to be rude, but I want to get Otis into the truck."

"No problem." She followed him to the truck.

When he shut the passenger side door, she was standing behind it. "No," he said, trying not to be rude. "We're not having a party. But I sold a song today, so people just stayed late to have some cake."

"I see." She leaned against his truck, allowing her sweater to slip off her bare shoulder. "Would you like to come over to The Purple Oasis for something to wash that cake down with?"

This was ridiculous. He was going to have to be firm, even if it hurt her feelings or offended her. "Willow, you seem to be a lovely woman, but I'm just not interested in anything beyond neighborly friendship with you."

She stood up straight. She was offended. Or mad? He couldn't really tell. Maybe both. "You sure seemed interested when you kissed me!"

Hadn't that been the other way around? He was pretty sure *she'd* kissed *him*. "I'm sincerely sorry if I gave you the wrong impression."

"Is there someone else?"

"No," he snapped. "This isn't about anyone else. I'm just not interested. Now, if you'll excuse me."

She probably would've said more if he'd given her a chance, but he didn't. Moving as fast as possible, he got into the truck and started the engine. She hadn't moved. He drove away, and when he looked in his rearview mirror, she was still standing there, her arms folded across her chest, staring at the back of his truck. Why were women so complicated?

When he finally got home, he spent a few minutes outside so that Otis could do his business, and then they headed inside and straight to bed. But despite his exhaustion and the soft sheets, he couldn't quite fall asleep. Hannah's face kept drifting through his thoughts. She'd looked so sad when he'd criticized her hugging. Why had he done that? Why couldn't he have kept his mouth shut? True, he'd been trying to help, but he sure had botched the job.

Maybe he didn't have to wait for tomorrow. Maybe he should call and apologize right now. It was awfully late, though. He looked at his phone's clock. Yep. Definitely too late to call.

But another half hour crawled by and he still couldn't sleep. If he didn't get this settled, he was going to be up all night. He had to call her. He had to get this sorted. True, she'd be irritated with him if he woke her up, but she was already irritated with him. Before he could talk himself out of it again, he hit the green call button.

After three rings, a groggy hello greeted him. Of course, he'd woken her up. Had he really expected otherwise? "Hannah, I'm so sorry to call so late, but I really need to apologize to you."

"Who is this?" Really? She didn't recognize his voice? Had she gotten into the wine again?

"Uh ... it's Logan. Logan Hawkins." He included his last name to be funny. Or just in case.

There was a few seconds of silence. "Then why does my phone say Gomer Pyle is calling?"

He snorted a laugh. "Sorry, didn't plan on a late night phone call when I did that."

"Oh ... uh ... okay." She was confused.

"Anyway. It's not Gomer Pyle. It's Logan, and I won't keep you long. I just wanted to apologize for today. I was an idiot, and I'm sorry if I freaked you out or offended you. I should have asked permission before hugging you."

She didn't say anything. Had she fallen back to sleep?

"Hannah?"

"Sorry ... it's okay. I didn't think you had anything to apologize for. You don't." She sounded more awake now.

He let out a long breath. That was a relief. "Okay, good. Then I'm doubly sorry I called—"

"No, no, don't be."

"It just seemed like you didn't want to be hugged, and I know that some people don't like people touching them, and then I was worried that I offended you because I critiqued your hug and asked you to try again, to do a better job." Describing his own behavior made him feel like even more of a jerk.

"That's not the way I saw the situation."

Oh good. "How did you see it?"

There was a long silence, and he wished he hadn't asked. He was about to recant the question when she spoke.

"Logan, I've got so much going on in my mind, I have no idea how to communicate any of it." She took a deep breath. "I don't want to freak you out, but ... you know what? Never mind. It's late, and I'm tired, so I don't want to try to communicate clearly right now. But just know that you didn't do anything wrong, and I appreciated your hug. I do like hugs, I promise. Thanks for calling, though. Have a good rest of your night."

"Yeah. You too. Good night, Hannah." He waited for her to say something else, but she hung up.

He had thought he would feel better after apologizing, but he didn't. He was even more confused now. What had she been about to tell him? What did she think might freak him out?

Chapter 29

Hannah poured herself a third cup of coffee. She hadn't gotten much sleep the night before. She'd been sleeping like a baby until Logan had called, but after that, she'd lain awake until her alarm. She still couldn't believe he'd called her, that he'd cared enough about her feelings to call her in the middle of the night to apologize. Nor could she believe she'd almost confessed her feelings to him. That had been a close call. She had thought she might feel better if she came clean, but she had to work with this man. She had to see him every day. So she had decided it would be smarter to keep her feelings to herself until they went away.

She turned to head back to her office. She'd kept her door shut all day, trying to avoid contact. She hoped that the old adage "out of sight, out of mind" would prove true for her.

Only minutes later, Suzette called everyone to the front room. Grudgingly, Hannah left the sanctity of her office and headed down the hallway toward the common area, where she found Logan sitting with his guitar. He smiled at her, and she quickly dropped his gaze, and then felt guilty for not returning his smile. She took a chair as far away from him as possible.

"Thanks for coming, everyone," Suzette said, looking particularly chipper. She'd obviously gotten plenty of sleep. "I don't know why we didn't think of this last night, but Alex mentioned that she hasn't even heard Logan's song yet. I figured this might be true for others, so I asked Logan to sing it for us."

Logan yawned and somehow managed to look handsome while he did so. Of course, the yawn was contagious, and Hannah followed suit, certain she looked far less attractive than he had, and covering her mouth with one hand as best she could.

"If you're not too tired," Suzette said, sounding a smidge sarcastic.

"Sorry, I didn't get much sleep last night." He started playing an intro. "But of course, I'm happy to oblige. Here's the song. It'll sound much better once Branch does it." Logan began to sing, and Hannah thought her heart might melt into a puddle. "Has the helter-skelter of every day got you down? You're not alone in this dog eat dog town. But we aren't rats, weren't designed for the rat race ... sprinting toward death at a break-neck pace." She hadn't remembered Logan's voice being so moving. His eyes were closed, and she could tell he believed in every word he sang. "What if the best page is somewhere in the middle ... what if we slowed down a little ... if you rush to the end, you miss the whole book."

Is that what she was doing? Was she missing pages of her own story? She didn't believe that she was rushing toward death. That idea seemed a little extreme, but she was certainly rushing, and what if he was a little bit right? What if she was missing things along the way? She didn't want to be like Logan, without a care in the world. She had goals. She had things she wanted to accomplish in life. But maybe she didn't have to be in *so much* of a hurry. Maybe Logan had a *small* point. Maybe she could slow down a little, try to find a better balance.

Logan's volume picked up as he headed into his hook. "There are fields and fields of them, if you only take the time to look ... smile, slow down, take notice ... and stop and smell the roses."

The second verse was even more powerful. He talked about getting to the end and looking back, and wondering what it was all for. His words, or maybe it was his voice, or maybe the synergy of the two, sent chills up her arms. This was such a good song. He deserved the success it was giving him. He repeated the chorus, and Suzette's lips moved along with the lyrics. She'd obviously heard the song a few times. The bridge was more upbeat, and Hannah found herself tapping her toes.

"Live a little, live a little, life is found in the little moments, big things happen in the little moments." He looked up at her the second time he sang the words, his eyes sparkling, and flashed her a big smile before launching into the chorus for the final time.

When he finished, everyone stood and applauded, and Hannah was so proud of Logan, so sincerely happy for him, that tears came to her eyes. He put his guitar down and strode toward her, and before she realized what was happening, he was wrapping his long arms around her and squeezing her. What was he doing? What was everyone going to think of this? He gently pushed her head into his chest and whispered, "Just relax. Let me hug you for a second."

She tried to relax her body and found it wouldn't respond.

Not letting go of her, he chuckled. "That's a little better. Now breathe."

She inhaled and almost swooned at how amazing he smelled. Then she let out a long breath and felt some of the tension ride out of her on that breath.

"There you go," he whispered into the top of her head. Then he let go of her and grabbed her hand. He opened his body up to the rest of them and said, "I should tell you all that Hannah inspired this song."

Her cheeks got hot. Was he seriously announcing to everyone that he thought she was rushing toward death?

But no one looked surprised at his announcement. Maybe they all thought that too.

Chapter 30

It had felt so good to hold Hannah. And she had relaxed in his arms—a little. He'd made the right decision, then. When he'd realized Hannah was avoiding him, he'd decided the best thing he could do was to hug her as soon as he saw her. He didn't know what was going on with them exactly, but if nothing else, he wanted to have a real friendship with her.

That's what he'd thought. But holding her had made him think he wanted even more. What would she say to that? He had no idea. Now, back in his office, alone with Otis, he thought he needed to ask her out on a real date. And the sooner the better. Except that he didn't want to leave Otis alone. Otis was scheduled for what would probably be his final chemo treatment on Friday. But Otis usually didn't feel well afterward, and his reactions were unpredictable. Once he'd gotten sick the very next day. Once, it had been a week after the treatment. Logan didn't know how to predict it, and didn't want to ask a dog-sitter to deal with it.

He didn't think Hannah would mind having Otis along on a date, but what kind of a date could he bring them both on? Certainly not a fancy restaurant or a show. A trip to the park would be too stimulating for Otis, and he wasn't supposed to be around other dogs. Inviting Hannah into his home would probably be too forward. But Logan didn't want to wait until Otis was better.

The drive-in! The idea popped into his mind with a bang. He hadn't thought of it because he'd never even been to a drive-in movie. There wasn't a drive-in in Nashville, but there was one in Watertown. That was quite a drive, but it was okay. It would give them some time to talk. He jumped out of his chair and headed toward Hannah's office.

"Come in!" she called after he knocked. Her voice sounded funny.

He opened the door to find Hannah at her computer, crying. "What's wrong?" He did *not* like the sight of her in tears.

She shook her head and wiped at her eyes. "Nothing. It's stupid."

He pulled a chair over so he could sit beside her. "It's not nothing, because you're crying."

She rolled her eyes and wiped at them again. "I just feel so stupid." She smiled. "Really, it's nothing. Maggie Hammer turned down my song, which," she hurried to add, "I think is a good thing. I'm not crying because she turned the song down. I'm crying because I'm just ..." She waved at her own face as if that could make her tears dry up and vanish.

He was so confused.

"I'm just feeling a little overwhelmed right now. I'm super tired and I always get overly emotional when I'm tired."

Oops. The tired part was probably his fault.

She did that weird little wave again. He couldn't see how that was helping, but if it made her feel better. "Got a lot going on in my head right now, but I'm really not sad about her turning it down. I knew it would happen, and I'm glad it happened, because I don't know if I even believe in the song anymore." She took a ragged breath, and then smiled at him. "You've kind of messed with my whole world view here, Logan. Gotta say, I never saw that coming." She suddenly seemed to notice that Otis wasn't with him. "Is Otis okay?"

He nodded. "Yeah. He's fine. He's sleeping. Are you sure you're okay?" Now was not the best time to ask her out.

"Yeah." She exhaled again, and her shoulders fell. "I'm good. I'm just a little emotionally overwhelmed."

He wondered what else was going on in her mind. "Want to talk about it?"

She stared at him as if contemplating: did she want to share with him? Apparently, she decided against it, because she shook her head. "Nah, I'll be okay, I promise. Sometimes it's just not easy being me."

He could imagine. "Okay, well, let me know if you do want to talk about it. Maybe we could write it out."

She smiled broadly, knowing exactly what he meant. He wasn't much for processing his emotions through songs, but he knew scores of songwriters worked in exactly that way.

"Yeah, maybe that would be a good idea."

He stood to go.

"What did you need?"

"Huh?"

"You came in here for something, and it wasn't to ask why I was crying. Unless of course you could hear me from your office."

"Oh ..." Should he do what he'd come here to do? He still wanted to ask her out, but it didn't seem like a good time now. Plus, she was obviously feeling very vulnerable, and he didn't want her to feel pressured into anything. Maybe she needed a friend right now more than she needed a date. "Sorry, I don't remember."

She smiled, her eyes dry now. "Okeedoke. Well, if you remember, come on back."

Chapter 31

Hannah couldn't believe Logan had caught her sobbing at her computer. She could hardly believe she'd *been* sobbing at her computer. She didn't usually have such emotion-volcanoes, but, like she'd told Logan, she was overtired.

The volcano had started with that hug. It had felt so good to be in his arms. She couldn't remember ever feeling like that with a man. Of course, no man had ever really taken the time to hold her.

So now her brain was sprinting around the hamster wheel. Should she play it safe, avoid rejection by never acting on these feelings? She was now fairly sure they weren't going to go away on their own. They were too strong. Or should she come clean, get rejected, and then start the recovery process, like the dozen times before? Maybe. But could she still work with him after being rejected by him? She didn't think so. And that meant finding another publisher. She didn't want to do that. She didn't want to leave Suzette. She didn't want to leave Logan.

So she wouldn't. She would keep her feelings to herself. This would make good fodder for songs about unrequited love, and that would be it.

As for the rest of her emotional lava, yes, Logan had a point. She *would* try to slow down a little. She would force herself to relax. She just had to figure out a way to do that. What did she enjoy doing other than working?

Nothing.

She was a terrible swimmer, so water activities terrified her. She liked being outdoors, but not if there were bugs, so camping and hiking wouldn't work. She'd gotten a pedicure once and the resulting toenail injury had put her in the ER, so no more of that. She used to help her mother with the gardening, but her mother had eventually banned her from the gardens because she was killing everything. Yoga? Maybe, but that sounded painful. Maybe she should take up golf. Nah, she wasn't athletic. She'd be terrible at it. And who would she golf with? People didn't golf alone, did they?

Maybe she needed more friends. But that sounded like a lot of work. That wouldn't be relaxing at all.

Maybe she needed her own Otis. Her heart leapt at the thought. Maybe that *was* it! That would certainly bring more joy into her life, and she would be forced to slow down to meet that dog's needs. She'd been wanting a dog since she left her parents' dogs behind, but she'd always thought she didn't have enough time. And until recently, she really hadn't had the funds either. But now she had the funds; so, she would make the time. She'd have to take her dog on walks, and go to the park. She never went on walks unless she was going somewhere, and then it was speed walking. And she'd never been to any of Nashville's parks.

This was it. What a great idea! She couldn't wait to tell Logan. She jumped up to leave, but then thought she'd better stop and check her makeup first, having only recently recovered from waterworks.

Five minutes later, with mascara reapplied and other makeup repaired, she headed back down the hall.

"Good grief, you two should start sharing an office," Chloe muttered as she passed, and Hannah's strides slowed as she felt self-conscious.

Don't read too much into it. Those words didn't have to mean anything, she told herself, but she was still shaken when she reached Logan's door. He was lying on his couch with Otis, both of them hard at work. He turned his head toward her and gave her a lazy smile. "I was just thinking about you."

He was? What did that mean? She didn't know but it caused an awkward hesitation on her part.

"Are you okay?

"Absolutely," she said too quickly. "I have great news, and I wanted to share it with you. Actually, I wanted your advice." She hadn't realized this was true until she'd said it.

Logan sat up, causing Otis to slide off his chest and onto his lap, but Otis seemed happy where he landed. "What's up?"

She widened her stance, put her hands on her hips, and pointed her chin up. "I've decided to get a puppy."

He barked out a short, incredulous laugh. "A puppy? Where did this come from?"

"Your song," she said in a mock-accusing tone.

He gave another single-syllable bark-laugh. "My song? I don't remember mentioning puppies in any of my songs."

"You didn't, but you tell me to slow down and smell the roses, and I don't have any roses, so I'm choosing puppy breath instead."

The laughter left his eyes, so he no longer looked amused, but he still looked happy. "Are you sure you want a puppy? They're a lot of work. You have to be with them a lot to house-train them, so you either have to run home during work, or bring him to work. I'm not sure Alex wants that many dogs in the building." His tone made it clear he didn't really care what Alex wanted.

"What are you saying?" Did he think she couldn't take care of a puppy?

He shrugged and motioned toward his chair.

She sat down.

"I'm not saying anything, really. Just thinking out loud. I think grown dogs can be easier, but there are also a million reasons to get them while they're young, and if you want a puppy, I'll be glad help. Otis too."

Otis made no move to confirm this promise.

She smiled at Otis, even though he wasn't looking at her. She was surprised at how attached she'd grown to him in such a short time. "How's he doing?"

Logan looked down at him with the eyes of a proud dad. "Great!"

"How many more chemo treatments does he need?"

"They're thinking just one, and then wait and see how it goes, but the doc is optimistic." He looked up. "But enough about my dog. Let's talk about yours. Are you thinking about rescuing? Or do you want a purebred with papers? Do you know what breed you want?"

Overwhelmed, she put her hand up to stall his questions. "That's why I need you. I have no idea what I want. And I do think I want a puppy. They're so cute! But I'd still be happy to get a rescue pup, if we can find one." She cringed at her use of the word *we*. He hadn't yet promised to help her *find* the dog. She was sure he would, but she didn't want to presume aloud.

But he didn't bat an eye. "Sure. I'm still friends with the woman who helped me find Otis."

A pang of jealousy stabbed at Hannah, and she dismissed it. It was ridiculous to be jealous of the man for having friends.

"Facebook friends, I mean," he said quickly, and Hannah worried that he'd seen her jealousy on her face. "She works for Forever Home Tennessee, and I'm sure she has puppies. What size dog do you want?"

Hannah thought. It might be nice to have a giant dog who could scare off bad guys. But it might be nice to have a cuddly lap dog too. She frowned. "I don't know."

"Don't know or don't care?"

She didn't know the answer to this either. "I don't know."

He chuckled. "You live in an apartment, right?"

She nodded. "But it's a big apartment." This might have been an exaggeration.

"And some people have to worry about dog food expense. Big dogs eat more, but you probably don't have to worry about that, since you're a rich and famous songwriter." He laughed.

She knew he was kidding around, but she still enjoyed his over-the-top praise.

"Small dogs live longer, and they're easier to fly with. You can't fit a Great Dane under the seat in front of you. Big dogs can offer protection for you, but they also shed more, if you care about that."

She did care about that. She liked her apartment neat and tidy. She hated for that to be a deciding factor; it made her feel small. "Let's go small."

He laughed. "Small it is. Do you care about male or female?"

"I don't think so. Should I?"

"Not for any reason I can think of. Are you sure about this? I can call Karen right now."

Ah, the rescue woman had a name, and it was Karen. "I'm sure. Are you sure they'll let me adopt? Don't I have to apply and get in line and all that?"

"Yes, but I'll recommend you, so that should speed things up." He pulled his phone out of his pocket. "Actually, I don't have her number, so I'll Facebook her first, and then call."

Oh good. At least he didn't have Karen's phone number.

Chapter 32

L ogan had been trying to think of a first date, and then it had fallen into his lap. They were going to the animal shelter. Not exactly wine and roses, but he found it strangely appropriate for them—and she even let him drive. He tried to get Otis to stay in the crew cab, but he wouldn't comply. As soon as Logan clicked his seatbelt, Otis climbed into Hannah's lap. The dog had good taste.

Hannah let out a little squeal, though Logan didn't know if it was a squeal of delight or merely one of surprise, but she didn't push him off. She patted him until he lay down on her lap, and then kept running her hand down his back after that. Logan found himself a bit jealous of his dog.

"How far is it?"

"Not far at all. In Madison. Want to listen to some music?"

"Sure. What do you have?"

"Um ... I've got some songs on my phone, but I usually just listen to the radio."

"Oh, sure. Perfect."

He pressed a button on his steering wheel and a familiar voice filled the cab.

Hannah groaned. "The song is so lame." Her eyes snapped toward him. "Wait, you didn't write this one, did you?"

He laughed. "Nope. I can't take credit for this little ditty."

She blew out a puff of air, and one of Otis's ears twitched. "Good thing. That would have been more foot in mouth than I could deal with right now."

He wished then that he had told her it was his song. He did wish he'd written it. It was getting a ton of airplay. "You can change the station."

"No thanks. The next song will be better."

It wasn't. She complained about that one too. She was a tough critic, hard to please. But somehow this made him feel better. He'd known that she wasn't all that impressed with his work. Now he knew it wasn't just him. She wasn't impressed with most songs. "What do you want out of this career? I mean, really. Be honest."

Her jaw dropped a little. It was cute. "Wow, look at Logan Hawkins starting a serious conversation."

"If you're going to make everything a joke, then never mind."

She tipped her head back and giggled. Finally, he'd made her laugh—and he'd done so by acting like her.

"I want to be successful. I know that's kind of ambiguous. When I decided to come to Nashville, I got a lot of flak. So I guess I want to prove those naysayers wrong. I want the big writing credits, and I know it sounds shallow, but I want the awards. But more than that, I want to write real songs. Not that your songs aren't real," she rushed to add. "Especially your newest one. Obviously, that's real. I mean, I guess there's a place for silly little songs that don't really say anything, but I want to write new melodies with poetic lyrics that really say something. Even if it's something that's been said before, I want to say it in a new way." She looked at him. "Does that make sense?"

It did, and he told her as much. "I just want to make lots of money," he said, answering a question she hadn't asked.

"I know, and I get that. Honestly, that was never on my mind in the beginning, but now that I've experienced a little bit of the financial benefits, you're right. That part is cool."

Logan and Hannah were standing on a small patch of common ground, and Logan liked the feel of it.

Some commercials gave way to a new song and Hannah asked if she could turn it up.

"You don't have to ask permission. You do what you gotta do."

She turned the volume knob and smiled. "Thanks. I love this song."

"I love all Jamey Johnson's songs."

She raised an eyebrow. "Really? I didn't even know if you liked music."

He barked out a laugh. "Don't be ridiculous. Of course I like music."

Her eyes were sparkling, and it occurred to him that she might be messing with him. He waited for the song to end and then said, "You probably already know this, but I just want to put it out there. You don't have to get a dog today. If you don't see one that you connect with, this isn't your last chance or anything. I know you're eager, but I also think you'll feel a connection when you meet the dog you're supposed to take home."

"You mean like a spark?"

He chuckled. "What?"

She let out a long breath and stared out the windshield. "My mom always used to say not to just go for the handsomest guy or the smartest guy but to wait until I felt a spark with someone."

"Yeah, I guess. Something like that. So did you?"

"Did I what?"

"Find a guy that made you feel a spark?"

She didn't answer, at first. Then all she said was, "Maybe."

Maybe? What did that mean? That she didn't know? Or that she didn't want to tell him? Either way, that was a pretty weird thing to say.

Chapter 33

Why oh why did I say the stupid spark thing? Hannah hadn't been thinking. That had been something that her mother had said to her over and over, and no, she'd never really felt anything resembling a spark with someone—until very recently. And she hadn't realized that she *was living* the spark in that exact moment until she said it out loud. Why had she chosen to open up about *that* little detail of her upbringing? Because she'd been an odd combination of nervous and comfortable, and she'd been blabbering.

And now, in an attempt to *stop* blabbering, she'd been silent, and Logan was looking at her every thirty seconds as if he was sure something was wrong with her.

Maybe something was. She felt like she might be losing her mind.

He opened the door to the animal shelter for her, and she was hit by an awful smell: a horrific combination of wet dog and Clorox. She tried to breathe through her mouth, but then she could taste bleach on her tongue.

A symphony of barks greeted them, but there wasn't a dog in sight. A pretty woman behind a counter said, "Hey, Logan! Thanks so much for coming in!" She came around the counter and offered Hannah her hand.

Hannah, who wasn't usually terribly observant, noticed a wedding band on her other hand. That was comforting.

"You must be Hannah! I'm so glad you're thinking about adopting a dog!"

Adopting. The word sent a thrill streaking through her gut. She was going to adopt someone. She was going to do a good thing.

"Any particular traits you're looking for?"

Hannah thought for a second. "I'd like him to be house trained and I'd like him to like me back."

Karen's mouth opened wide for a laugh, revealing a large set of perfect teeth. Now that Hannah knew she was married, she was starting to like her. "I'm sure he or she is going to like you very much. So tell me about you, then. Are you home a lot? Are you really active?"

"Uh ... neither?"

Karen's smile faded a little. "Okay."

Hannah felt the need to defend herself. "I work a lot, but I can bring my dog to work." She didn't yet know if this was true, but Logan didn't correct her. "And no, I'm not very active, but I promise to take him on walks."

"So, you'll need one who will walk on a leash well enough to not drag you down the street."

Drag me down the street? Just what was she getting herself into here?

"I'm thinking low to medium energy, house trained, and not too big and strong?"

Hannah nodded. That sounded reasonable.

"Great. Would you like to meet some dogs?"

"Yes, please." Butterflies flitted around Hannah's stomach.

"Great. Right this way, please." Hannah and Logan followed her through a wooden door and into a large open area full of giant kennels. The barking tripled in volume.

"If you don't meet the right dog here," Karen hollered over the din, "we have some other dogs placed with foster families."

"Oh man, I shouldn't have come in here. I might end up going home with a second dog."

"We would certainly allow that!" Karen tittered.

The first dog they walked by jumped up and put his paws on the fence so that he was eye level with Hannah. She jumped back—straight into Logan's warm chest. "Ope, sorry." Her cheeks got hot.

"No problem." He touched her arm as she stepped away, and she couldn't quite figure out what had made that touch necessary.

The next dog had a bark that could've woken the dead. And the dead's dead ancestors. The dog was beautiful, but it was barking like it had treed a dinosaur. They moved on.

"You might like this one." Karen stopped in front of the third kennel. "He's only been with us a few weeks. We don't know much about his history, but he's a cute little thing. Some sort of terrier mix."

And he was cute. His whole body wiggled at their attention and his tail banged against the side of his kennel with an impressive tempo.

Hannah looked him over. "Can I pat him?" He was cute, but she was waiting for the spark.

"Of course."

As Karen unlocked the kennel door, Hannah caught movement out of the corner of her eye. In the back of the opposite kennel sat an adorable little hound dog with the saddest eyes. "Who's that?"

Karen looked over her shoulder, shutting the terrier's door again. "We call her Jackie. She's an older hound mix."

"She's beautiful." Hannah stepped closer to her kennel. "Can I pat her instead?" She felt guilty. "I mean, I'll pet the terrier too."

"Sure, you can try, but don't be offended. She's very skittish. She might not want you to pat her."

"That's okay."

Logan touched her arm again. "Are you sure? If she's scared of you, she might not be very affectionate. Plus, fearful dogs can be aggressive dogs."

"She's shown no signs of aggression with us, but he does have a point."

"Why's she so scared?" Hannah asked as Karen opened Jackie's door.

"Don't know. She was a stray, brought in about six months ago."

"Six months ago?" She'd been in that kennel for six months? Hannah stepped into the space, and Jackie backed up, wedging herself into the corner. Now that she was closer, Hannah could see the ring of gray fur around her muzzle. She knelt down and looked at the floor, holding her hand out so that Jackie could smell her.

"Good job!" Karen praised.

"Thanks. I grew up with dogs."

Jackie didn't move.

"Hey there, girl," Hannah said softly. "Can I pet you?"

Slowly, Jackie took a step forward. Hannah didn't stand up. She just continued holding her hand out. "I should have brought treats for you, shouldn't I? I'm sorry, Jackie, I didn't think of that. You deserve some treats, don't you?"

Jackie took two more steps and then sniffed Hannah's hand.

"Unreal," Karen said. She sounded very far away.

Jackie took another step and ran her head under Hannah's hand. "That's a good girl. It's nice to meet you too." Without looking at Karen, she asked, "Is there anything else I need to know about this one?"

"She is very skittish around strangers, so you'll have to be careful taking her places, but she is house trained, and she's very quiet. We don't know how old she is, maybe seven or eight, but we have seen no health issues. She's up to date on all her shots, of course." She clicked her tongue. "I've never seen her come to anyone so willingly. This is delightful."

"Looks like she and Hannah have a spark," Logan said.

Chapter 34

Logan couldn't stop grinning. Otis had been banished to the tiny backseat of the truck, and he wasn't happy about it, but there was a stinky hound dog at Hannah's feet acting as though she'd just won the lottery.

She had.

Logan's connections with the animal rescue hadn't excused Hannah from the mountain of paperwork, and it had taken her twenty minutes to work her way through it. Then they'd loaded Jackie up and headed home. But the dinner bell in Logan's stomach had rung hours ago. He cleared his throat. "Would you like to stop and get something to eat?" He strained to see her facial expression in the dark truck. Her hesitation made him nervous.

"The truth is, I'm starving, but I don't want to leave her alone in your truck. For lots of reasons."

He thought she'd be fine, but he wasn't going to argue.

"She might eat Otis."

He laughed heartily. They both already knew Jackie well enough to know that, if left alone with Otis, she would do her best to stay away from him. He thought maybe Hannah didn't want to leave Jackie for Hannah's own good, more than for Jackie's. "We could go to a Sonic? You wouldn't have to get out of the truck." Not exactly the fancy restaurant he'd envisioned for their first date, but this wasn't actually a date.

She gasped. "That's actually a great idea!"

"You don't have to sound so surprised that I could have a great idea."

She laughed and the sound reminded him of wind chimes.

He remembered when it had been so difficult to get her to crack a smile. What had changed? Was she just warming up to him? Or was she changing as a person? Was he the one changing her? He shook his head. That was an arrogant thought. He was just getting to know the real Hannah now. At least, he hoped this one was the real one, and the uptight, cranky one was the facade.

"I'm genuinely excited. I usually try to eat healthy, but I really love their chili cheese tots."

His surprised laugh sounded more like a cough, and he covered his mouth. "Chili cheese tots it is, then. There's probably a good chance Jackie has never had one of those."

Hannah turned toward him in the dark. "I don't know if I should feed her people food. Didn't I just pledge to take good care of her and keep her healthy?"

"You did. Healthy and *happy*. I don't think a single chili cheese tot is going to hurt her, and I think it will make her very happy."

They stopped talking for a while, and Hannah sang along with the radio so quietly that Logan had to strain to hear her. At one point, he caught himself holding his breath so he could hear her better.

Just when he thought he might faint from hunger, they pulled into the Sonic. Jackie picked her drooly jaw up off Hannah's knee to look up at the bright lights on the awning overhead. "What would you like besides the tots? Burger? Corn dog? My treat."

She hesitated again. "I'm pretty hungry, so you don't have to treat. I'll have two orders of tots and an All-American Dog with no onions." She started rifling through her purse.

"Seriously. I'm not going to let you pay for this, so don't bother trying. Do you want anything to drink?"

"Yes, please. Large Ocean Water."

"Ocean Water? Sounds salty." He laughed.

She didn't. "It's like pina colada soda."

He snickered. "Soda."

"Sorry, I'm from Maine, remember? It tastes like a pina colada *coke*. Is that better?"

"Yes, much better. Thank you."

A voice welcomed him to Sonic and asked what he'd like to have. He relayed Hannah's order and then topped it off with two corn dogs, a third chili cheese tots, and a peanut butter shake.

After the voice thanked him, Hannah said, "Why'd you laugh when I ordered chili cheese tots if you like them too?"

He didn't know the answer to that. Why had he laughed, exactly? Because Hannah made him nervous? He couldn't exactly admit to that. Well, he *could*, but he wasn't going to. "I don't know. It just wasn't what I was expecting." He slid his card into the slot below the order screen.

"What were you expecting?"

"I don't know." He suddenly felt very, very stupid. "Did you know that Sonic was originally called Top Hat?"

"I did not know that." She sounded amused. "Why do you know that?"

He couldn't remember how he knew that. He tapped his temple. "This brain is a steel trap. Then the founder found out that Top Hat was trademarked, so he changed it to Sonic."

She dropped her jaw with exaggerated drama and said in a weird fake also exaggerated southern accent, "You mean we're supporting plagiarism by dining here?"

This was an absurd thing to say, and she'd said in an absurd manner, but he greatly appreciated her willingness to be silly with him. "Yes. Very much so." He raised his fist into the air. "Bring back plagiarism! Support plagiarism!"

She laughed as though he was the funniest man on the planet.

"Be careful, Hannah. I could get used to this."

The smile fell off her face as if a curtain of seriousness had fallen from her forehead. "Used to what?"

"Used to you thinking I'm funny. I've been trying to make you laugh for a while now, and I've usually failed—"

"That's not true," she said quickly. "I laughed at those stupid newsletter subscriptions. I haven't even unsubscribed from the German one yet. I laugh every time it pops into my inbox."

He raised an eyebrow. "Or is it that you can't find the unsubscribe button because you can't read German?"

She narrowed her eyes. "I'm pretty sure I'm smart enough to Google the German word for unsubscribe if I wanted to." She glanced down at Jackie, who was staring up at her worshipfully. "So, what other random facts do you know about Sonic?"

He thought for a few seconds, feeling a little desperate to impress her. "Um ... they dip their onion rings in vanilla ice cream."

"What?" she shrieked and Jackie jerked her head back in fear. Hannah leaned closer to the dog and rubbed both ears. "I'm sorry, sweetie. Didn't mean to scare you." Then she looked at Logan. "Why didn't we order onion rings, then?"

"It's not too late." He was grinning like a fool. He couldn't stop.

They were quiet for a few minutes until a carhop appeared beside his open window.

"Good evening!"

Her response resembled a snarl. Wordlessly, she handed him his food through the window.

"Thank you." He handed one of the drinks over to Hannah and realized the cranky carhop had started to wheel away. "Wait!" he cried after her.

She wheeled back, coming to an abrupt halt just inches from his elbow. Her face screamed annoyance.

He handed her a folded up five. "You forgot your tip."

She reached out and took the money, tentatively, as if he was only teasing and was going to yank it away from her at the last second.

Of course, he didn't.

After a few dumbfounded seconds, something resembling a smile tickled her lips. "Thank you."

"You're welcome."

In a better mood, she wheeled away.

"That was weird," Hannah said.

"Yes, it was. Sonic carhops are usually super friendly. That's sort of their shtick."

"No. Well, that too, but I meant it was weird that you just tipped her. Are people supposed to tip at Sonic?"

He shrugged. "I don't know. I tip everywhere."

Chapter 35

Hannah couldn't stop thinking about her evening with Logan. She'd had the best time with him. If it had been a date, which it hadn't been, it would have definitely been the best date ever.

She had to admit it. She really liked him. She more than liked him. She could hardly believe it. She liked him so much that she was willing to gamble. Yes, there was a good chance that he would reject her, but anyone who would tip a rude carhop at a fast food joint would at least let her down gently. She knew now that he was a genuinely nice guy. She hadn't known that before. She'd mistaken his confidence for arrogance.

But maybe he wouldn't reject her. He'd told her she was beautiful. And he'd been so nice to her, helping her to find and adopt Jackie, and buying her dinner. Or maybe he'd done all that just because he was a nice guy. She didn't know.

She did know that she liked him and she had to get it off her chest or it was going to drive her crazy. Besides, at the very least, she thought he'd be flattered, and she wanted to make him feel good about himself, even though he seemed to have no trouble in that department.

But *how* to tell him? She wasn't much of a flirt. Should she just come right out and say it? Should she send him a text? An email? A more confident, romantically inclined woman would write him a song, but she didn't have that in her. Should she just ask him out?

She felt like she was back in junior high, complete with the butterflies and the nervous sweating. At least the acne had stayed in the past.

It wasn't until she'd finally left her office to take Jackie into the backyard for a potty break that she had an idea.

She would prank him.

He would love it.

The idea made her giddy. It would be fun, it would be funny, and it would make him feel special.

Now the only problem was that she had no idea how to prank someone. She looked down at Jackie who was now rolling around on her back as if she'd never encountered grass before. She was ecstatic. "I guess we can stay out here a few more minutes," she said softly.

Jackie ignored her.

"Come on Jacks, help me think of a prank. How do you romantically prank a prankster?"

Jackie continued to ignore her. She cared way more about the grass massage that the ground was currently giving her back than she did about her new mom's love life.

Hannah sat down on the picnic table bench and thought, but came up with nothing. She was really bad at this. She did not have a mischievous bone in her body. Too bad she couldn't borrow one of Logan's. She took out her phone and searched for "romantic prank ideas." The results quickly told her that this wasn't a thing. Apparently no one, anywhere in the world, used practical jokes to communicate a crush.

Maybe she should write him a song after all. A really, really *terrible* song. Full of all the worst, gushy, trite clichés she could think of. But would Logan even know they were cliché? He might think the song was awesome. Or maybe she should make him a mixed tape of terrible ushy-gushy songs. Again, he might like them.

She needed to walk around, get her blood moving. She gently yanked on Jackie's leash. "Come on, girl. Let's go for a stroll." Jackie grudgingly got up, but once they got going, her tail whipped back and forth like it was trying to put out a fire. They walked along the building and out onto the sidewalk. Hannah slowed and looked at Logan's truck. She didn't know why, but she had the urge to incorporate his truck in this scheme of hers.

But how?

She stopped walking and stared at the truck. Jackie sat down and stared at the truck too. Hannah could think of lots of goofy things to do to the truck, but none that conveyed the message she was trying to get across. Maybe this wasn't going to work. Maybe she had to come up with a more mature, less Logan-specific way to convey her feelings.

And then it came to her. Like a download from the heavens. She would paint it.

He would think his truck had been vandalized, and he would be horrified.

Years ago, her dad had done that to his own truck before taking them trick or treating, using a special paint that looked like spray paint but rubbed right off. Yes! This was the plan. She looked down at her new friend. "Sorry, girl. We're cutting the walk short." This was an understatement. They hadn't even started the walk yet.

She returned to her office to retrieve her keys and purse and then headed for the hardware store. She didn't know if they would have the paint she needed, but she felt like circumstances were aligning in her favor, so maybe they would.

Chapter 36

Logan's phone buzzed and he looked down to see a text from Suzie Q. He was wanted in her office. He didn't mind. He wasn't being very productive anyway. Leaving Otis behind, he strode down the hallway and then plopped down in a chair facing her. "What's up?"

She folded her hands across her lap. "Big news. Branch Bronson wants you to go out on the road with him for a little bit."

It took several seconds for that to sink in. "Seriously?"

She nodded. "Not for long. He's finishing up his tour and then he's coming back to finish up in the studio. But he was so impressed with your roses song that he wants to see if you guys can't work together to get a few more album cuts."

Logan opened his mouth to say something, but Suzie Q interrupted him. "Don't worry. I already asked. You can definitely bring your dog."

Logan hadn't even thought of Otis yet. This fact shocked him. Why hadn't Otis been the first thing on his mind?

Because Hannah had been.

The greatest singer in all of country music wanted him out on the road, wanted to write with him. This was the opportunity of a lifetime. He couldn't go, of course, because he wouldn't leave Otis. But that's not what had been on his mind. What had been on his mind was the fact that he didn't want to leave Hannah. He could hardly believe it. He liked her even more than he thought he did. Maybe he even more than liked her.

"I can't."

She nodded. "I thought you might say that."

"Do you think this will hurt me?"

"Nah," she quickly said. "Branch will understand."

"Understand what?" He hadn't given her a reason.

"He'll understand that there's someone here that you don't want to leave behind."

Was she talking about Otis? If so, why didn't she just say his name? Logan sat there speechless, feeling foolish.

"Do you want to take some time to think about it?"

He shook his head. "Please tell his people how much I appreciate the offer, and that I'll be happy to write with him when he's in Nashville."

She nodded. "Okay, I'll let him know."

He didn't like the look on her face, but he didn't dare ask her what it meant. "So, is that it?"

She nodded. "That's it."

He stood to go.

"Logan? I know it's none of my business, but I feel like you guys are my kids, and as your unofficial mother hen, I think you should tell her how you feel."

His cheeks got hot. He started to pretend that he didn't know what she was talking about, but then thought, why bother? He nodded. "Maybe."

She winked. "Just write her a song." Then she waved him out of her office.

He headed back down the hall. Under no circumstances could he write Hannah a song. He'd opened his big mouth about how all his songs were total hogwash, how he just said things that women wanted to hear so that he could sell records. Yes, these things were still true, but he wished he'd never said them to Hannah. Now if he *did* try to write a sincere love song, she'd never believe it. She'd think he was being smarmy. Nope. He wasn't going to write her a song. Instead, he had to act like a normal person. He had to simply ask her out on a date. The thought sent his stomach into somersaults. Would she say yes? Maybe?

He wasn't worried about his pride. That would survive rejection. He'd been rejected plenty of times before and it hadn't slowed him down a bit. But would his *heart* survive being rejected by Hannah? He liked the dream of her very much. If he tried to turn the dream into reality and he failed, he wouldn't even have the dream anymore. He'd be left with nothing but heartache and disappointment. All alone in his office, he smiled to himself. He'd be able to write heartbreak songs for the first time in his career. So maybe this situation was a win-win. Either he won Hannah or he won some new songwriting material.

He looked down at Otis and sighed, desperately hoping he ended up with the first option.

Chapter 37

Hannah's heart was trying to pound its way out of her chest. She felt as though she were committing an actual crime instead of an innocent prank. She was all alone in the street, but she felt a million accusing eyes watching her every move. The streetlight overhead had never seemed so bright. She looked over her shoulder for the umpteenth time before squatting to continue her paint job.

Originally, she'd planned to write, "Will you go out with me?" But then she'd decided that was too long, and opted for the shorter "Take me to dinner?" Right now, she was spelling out dinner, and the word was the longest word in the history of words. But when she hurried, the letters became illegible, and she had to force herself to slow down again. She'd never been much of a visual artist, and that was clear with this masterpiece. She took a deep breath and tried to steady her hand. The noxious fumes were making her queasy, and her eyes had been watering steadily since she'd painted the first T. She felt like she'd been cutting up onions for hours. The spray paint might not hurt the paint on Logan's truck, but she wondered what it was doing to her nervous system.

Halfway through the word *dinner*, she started to have doubts, and stopped painting. Then she laughed at herself. It was true that she could back out now, but she'd have to wipe off what she'd painted so far, and that would take longer than finishing the job. Logan would be outside soon. Did she want to be hiding in the shadows somewhere watching his reaction? Or did she want to be standing next to his truck furiously trying to scrub off those last letters? And if she did choose the second option, how was she going to explain herself?

Nope. It was too late. She was invested. She would finish the question, and then she would deal with the consequences. Either she'd get to out to dinner with a man she loved spending time with, or she'd be embarrassed. Either way, she'd live through it. She hoped.

Platinum's front screen door banged shut, and she heard the jingle of Otis's tags. It was so encouraging that he was walking around on his own power now and didn't need Logan to carry him everywhere. She finished the R at the end of *dinner*. The spray can suddenly seemed awfully loud. She hadn't done the question mark yet, but she could hear Logan's boots on the asphalt, getting closer and louder. She hesitated, losing precious seconds that she should've used to get to the shadowy line of trees along the sidewalk. She peeked up over the bed of his truck and gasped. He was *so close*. Much closer than she'd thought. Suddenly, she was terrified, and so, so certain that this had been a dreadful idea. Like a scared rabbit, she scurried around to the back of his truck and crouched, her cheek pressed against the tailgate.

"What the?" Logan's exclamation seemed incredibly loud in the still darkness, and Hannah jumped. He hadn't sounded amused. Maybe the prankster didn't like being pranked. Logan said a naughty word, and Hannah's heart sank. He was not impressed. This had been the worst idea of her life. "Are you kidding me?" he called out into the darkness. Who was he talking to? Did he know she was there?

"What?" a female voice answered. Who was that? Hannah stood up a little to look over the tailgate, but she couldn't see anyone. She squatted back down and looked under the truck. There were Otis's four feet, but Logan's boots weren't there anymore. He'd left Otis standing in the street?

"Don't play innocent. This isn't funny! How am I supposed to get that off?"

"Get what off?" Hannah recognized the voice: Willow.

Shoot. What should she do? Come out and come clean and let everyone know she'd lost her mind? Yes, that's exactly what she should do. She told her legs to move.

They did not obey.

Something tickled her dangling hand, and she almost shrieked. She looked down at Otis's wide eyes, which seemed to be asking her why she was crouching behind his master's truck. She had no answer for him.

"You painted my truck! You're going to pay to have that paint removed!"

"Logan, I didn't do—"

"Willow ..." His voice had quieted and grown gentler. "I thought we discussed this. I'm not interested in you. I have feelings for someone else."

He did? Who?

"Whatever!" Willow cried. "I'm not interested in you either. Man, how big is your ego?"

"Then why did you spray paint an order on my truck?"

An order? Hannah thought. *What order?*

"An order?" Willow said.

"Yes! You wrote, 'Take me to dinner.' It sure looks like an order, especially since it's written in giant black letters."

Oh shoot. I really should've added the question mark. She couldn't take it anymore. She popped up out of her hiding spot.

Neither of them noticed her. They were standing a few feet apart on The Purple Oasis's lawn. Willow looked beautiful in a long, flowing tie-dyed purple dress. Hannah could tell by looking at the back of him that Logan was angry. His back was straight, his hands on his hips.

"Yoo-hoo!" she called, trying to sound chipper and instead sounding ridiculous.

They both turned toward her. At first, neither of them said anything, and she started walking toward them, wishing the earth would open up and swallow her whole. Otis trailed along behind her for emotional support. Or maybe he didn't think it was safe to stand alone in the street.

"Sorry, Logan. It wasn't her." She held up both her hands. One of her hands still held the paint can. With the other hand, she gave him some jazz fingers. "Surprise! You've been pranked."

Willow rolled her eyes and turned to go back into the house, mumbling "pathetic" as she went.

Pathetic might be the right word.

Logan stared at her, his eyes wide. "Y ... y ... you?" He was having trouble talking.

"Yes, me. I thought it would be funny." She stopped walking when she came within six feet of him. Otis kept going and came to a heel position beside Logan's leg. Then he turned and sat, staring up at Hannah. What a traitor. "Sorry, I'm not very good at pranking. And it's not permanent—"

Logan exhaled dramatically.

"It'll wipe right off. And it wasn't supposed to be an order. I forgot the question mark. It was supposed to say, 'Take me to dinner?'" She made sure her voice came up at the end to emphasize the interrogative nature of the mock-vandalism. Then she stopped talking. Her throat was dry and scratchy. She no longer cared whether he said yes. She just wanted this to be over so she could start looking for a new job.

No one said anything for several seconds. Then, sounding incredulous, he said, "Are you asking me out?"

She faked a laugh. "Yeah, that was the idea."

His laugh didn't sound remotely fake. His laugh sounded as though he'd just seen the funniest thing on the planet. He laughed and laughed, whooping it up while she stood there wanting to die. He took off his hat and wiped at his forehead; apparently he was laughing so hard he was breaking a sweat. Then he came toward her, still laughing.

Chapter 38

"Of course I'll go out with you." Logan wanted to wrap his arms around her, pick her up off the grass, and spin her around, but something stopped him. Maybe his own lack of courage. He rubbed his hand over his mouth, trying to stop laughing, but he couldn't. This was an *awesome* prank, and from such a novice! He was so proud of her.

She looked terrified, and he was desperate to comfort her. He stepped closer, wondering how he could do so, trying to find the right words. When he got closer, he saw that she'd been crying. "Oh no!" He went to her quickly then, his inhibitions forgotten, and wrapped his long arms around her. It was like hugging a cold, stiff board, but he didn't care. He pulled her into his chest. "I'm so sorry, I didn't mean to make you cry."

Her whole body shook in response, and at first, he thought her body had been wracked with a sob, but then he heard a little giggle muffled by his chest. He pulled back a little so that he could see her face, and she was definitely laughing. What on earth?

She patted his chest. "I'm not crying, you big oaf. The spray paint fumes made my eyes water." She wiped at them and pulled away from him, still laughing.

"Oh, phew. I thought I'd scared you when I hollered at Willow." He looked at The Purple Oasis and shook his head. "Man, I thought she'd lost her mind." Then he looked at the truck. "But now that I know it was you, well, somehow it makes perfect sense. So yes, I would love to take you to dinner. Want to go to Sonic?"

He'd been kidding, but her face looked grave. "Right now?"

He chuckled. "Well we *could* go get a hot dog right now, if you want, but I'd also like to take you on a proper date. How about if I pick you up in an hour or so? I'll go drop Otis off. You go drop Jackie off. And then I'll take you someplace nice. What kind of food do you like, other than hot dogs and chili?"

She seemed puzzled by that question.

He tried to help. "Italian? Mexican? French?"

"I think you should pick," she blurted out, as if she were on a game show with no idea of the right answer and the timer was about to buzz.

"Okay, I'll pick. And you're okay with leaving the dogs home this time?"

She smiled broadly and nodded. "Sure. Just this once."

They stood there staring at each other and smiling for a minute.

"Okay, then. I'll see you soon." No part of him wanted to walk away from her, but he had to if he was ever going to get to the actual date.

Otis hesitated before following, and Logan wondered if Otis was also reluctant to leave Hannah behind.

He reached the truck and touched the top of the black T. It sure felt like real paint. He rubbed it with his thumb, and the paint easily smeared and then disappeared. Oh good. He'd wondered if she was crazy with her claim of disappearing paint. He knew he'd forgive her even if she was. But apparently, she wasn't crazy. It was actually washable spray paint.

He looked up and saw that she was still standing where he'd left her. It was difficult to see her face in the dim light, but he could tell she was smiling. "You actually pranked me."

"I actually did," she called back. "Are you impressed?"

"Very." That's one thing Hannah often did: impressed him. And now he had to drive across town with "Take me to dinner" on the side of his truck. Sure, he could take the time to wipe it all off right now, but he didn't want to. It was dark out. Maybe not a lot of people would notice. He looked at her again. "I've changed my mind."

Her smile faded and he hurried to add, "You're picking me up. I don't want to drive around in this any more than I have to."

"I don't know where you live."

He called out his address and then wondered how many people in The Purple Oasis had heard him. He probably didn't need to worry about Willow showing up at his door, though. He'd certainly offended her enough so she'd never be interested in him. He'd have to apologize for that later. Funny, though, how annoyed he'd been when he'd thought the painted message was Willow's doing, and how amused he'd been when he'd learned it had been Hannah's. He opened the truck door and waited for Otis to jump in. Then he followed suit, glancing at Hannah one more time before driving away.

This had all been far simpler than he'd thought it would be. He hadn't had to ask her out. She'd done it for him. He realized then that he liked a strong woman. He liked it very much.

Chapter 39

Hannah was in such a tizzy that she was almost panting. She knew she'd been this nervous before, but she couldn't remember when. Her first date ever? Probably not. The prom? Maybe. Her first piano recital? Probably. That one had been pretty bad. She'd almost thrown up on the stage. She didn't feel like throwing up now. She only felt hot and shaky, as if she needed to diffuse a bomb and was running out of time. Of course, this level of panic didn't make sense. She knew this. But she didn't know how to stop it.

She opened her closet door and surveyed her wardrobe, which, for the first time, seemed horrifically inept. What had she been thinking, buying clothes like these? She was staring at twenty versions of the same outfit. Blue jeans and blue shirts. Sure, some of the shirts had stripes and some had polka dots, but they were all still *very* blue. She had some scarves, but those were gray. She looked at Jackie, who was lying on her bed as if she'd been living there her whole life. "Do you think I have time to go buy a dress?"

Jackie didn't answer.

It didn't matter. Even if she did have time to buy a dress, which she didn't, she'd also have to buy nylons and shoes that went with the dress.

She had to make do with what she had. So, she pulled out her dressiest jeans and her snazziest blue shirt. This one was navy blue—quite daring. She put in earrings and then pulled her hair out of her tight bun. As it did every night, her scalp sang its relief as the blood began to flow freely. She massaged her own head and then looked in the mirror. Her hair looked crazy—giant waves crashing down in all directions. But it was going to have to be good enough. She had to touch up her makeup. Her mascara and eye liner was a black smeared mess.

It took her fifteen minutes and lots of eye makeup remover to get it right, and by then she was late. He'd said he'd pick her up in an hour, and though he'd later said she was driving, he hadn't changed the timeline part of the plan. She hated being late, and this increased her anxiety. She stopped at the door and looked at Jackie, who was whining so loudly it sounded like a cry for help. "Sorry, girl. I promise, I won't be gone long." Jackie whined louder and began to shake her rear end back and forth. Apparently, she believed that if she could just wag her tail hard enough, Hannah would change her mind. Hannah stooped to kiss her on the top of the head. "I'll be right back. You'll be fine." She threw her a dog biscuit and then stepped outside. But halfway down the hall she could still hear Jackie crying.

She turned around. When she opened the door, Jackie jumped on her with such force she almost knocked her down. "Fine. You can come, but you have to stay in the car, and you have to stay in the backseat." She reached inside to grab a leash off the hook by the door, and then she and Jackie walked side by side out of her apartment building.

Traffic was ridiculous. She'd finally gotten up the nerve to ask the man out and now she was going to die of starvation before ever reaching his door. When she was about thirty minutes late, her phone rang. She pressed the button on her steering wheel and said hello.

"Did you change your mind?" She could hear him smiling.

"No. Stuck in traffic."

"Well, we are in Nashville."

"Indeed. I'm sorry, I'll be there as soon as I can."

"No worries. Drive safely. I'm really enjoying the fact that you're late for something." So he knew how much she hated being late. Just how well did he know her?

"Very funny. I'll be right there." They said their goodbyes and she hung up and looked at Jackie, who was sleeping peacefully on the seat beside her. "Wish I could sleep while you drove." She ran a hand down the dog's back and then decided she didn't want to sleep, as that would wreak further havoc on her eye makeup she'd worked so hard on.

Chapter 40

Logan paced beside his window, enduring a strange concoction of nervousness and excitement. He didn't want her to get there, because he was nervous. He couldn't wait for her to get there, because he was excited. Otis sat staring at him, as if wondering when and how his best friend had lost his mind.

Finally, she pulled into his driveway and he hurried outside. As he approached the car, he saw some commotion through the windshield. It took him several seconds to realize what he was looking at.

He opened the door and slid into the warm front seat. Then he turned and looked at Jackie's dejected face. "Hi, Jackie." He looked at Hannah. "I thought we weren't bringing the dogs."

Hannah's cheeks were pink. She looked down at her steering wheel. "Sorry. She wouldn't take no for an answer."

Logan laughed to let her know he wasn't really upset. "So, how about Stephen's Steakhouse?"

Hannah gasped, which was exactly the reaction he'd been hoping for. "We'll never get in there!"

"We will. I have connections."

She stared at him.

"What?"

"Are you serious?"

"Yes. I've already called, and there's a table waiting for us."

"Good grief. You're spending your Branch Bronson money before you even get it."

He laughed. "Who said I was buying? You're the one who asked me out!"

The pink in her cheeks darkened.

He reached out and put his hand on hers. "I'm totally kidding. Of course I'm buying, and no, tonight is being paid for by 'You Won't Remember Me Tomorrow.'"

She looked appropriately horrified, which he enjoyed. He knew she hated that song. He couldn't blame her. He didn't like it much either, but it had made him a pile of cash. "We don't have to listen to it. We just have to reap its rewards."

A small smile appeared on her lips. "Okay, deal. I've never been there, but I've heard it's amazing. I thought you had to call weeks in advance to get a table."

"It is delicious, and you do have to call weeks in advance, unless you're me." He puffed out his chest. "Or someone equally as important as me."

She rolled her eyes. "If you say so." She put the car in reverse and started backing out of his driveway.

He stayed silent to let her concentrate, even though it was hard to hold in his nervous chatter. When she got the car straightened out and headed in the right direction, he said, "You look nice."

She made a *pfft* sound, obviously not believing him.

"Do you have trouble accepting compliments?"

She hesitated. "Maybe."

"Well, I don't think I've ever seen your hair down, and it's absolutely gorgeous."

"Thank you," she said softly.

How could someone this professionally and intellectually confident be so unsure of herself socially?

"I'm really glad you asked me to do this. Thank you. I was going to ask you, eventually. I was just trying to decide how to do it."

She glanced at him and then quickly turned her eyes back to the road. "Really?"

"Really. And I don't think, no matter how long I took to come up with a way, I would have ever thought of spray painting your car."

She snickered. "I was trying to freak you out. Make you think someone had vandalized your truck. But then when you really thought that, I was so scared. You were really mad and I felt so bad. I don't think I'm cut out for pranking."

He smiled. "I don't think you are either, but I appreciate your efforts. And if you do decide you'd like to become a better prankster, I'd be happy to train you."

She laughed and he was again reminded of wind chimes. He couldn't believe how *right* it felt to be with her, as if this had always been the plan. Somehow, they just fit together, like two puzzle pieces that, when snapped together, gave the most satisfyingly snug connection. She was staring at him, and he wondered how long he'd been quiet, woolgathering about puzzle pieces. "Do you know how to get there?"

"I do."

"Terrific. If you go to the back entrance, there's valet service."

"I know that too."

"Sorry, I thought you might not, because you haven't been there."

"Just because I haven't been there doesn't mean I haven't gazed at the place longingly while driving by."

He laughed. "Well, tonight you can gaze at it longingly from the inside."

Chapter 41

The interior of Stephen's Steakhouse was everything she'd dreamed it would be. The carpet was so soft beneath her shoes that she wanted to take those shoes off and curl her toes into its softness. An eclectic collection of abstract art adorned the walls, and she knew that any one of those paintings cost more than a house. Crystal chandeliers provided a soft lighting that somehow accentuated the light provided by the candles on the tables. The host showed them to their table and pulled out her chair. She sat, feeling out of place but so happy to be there just the same. With trembling fingers, she unfolded the cloth napkin, which felt like silk.

"Nice, isn't it?" Logan said. "Actually, it's better than nice, and it's a good thing, because we'll be here a while."

A pang of jealousy jabbed at her chest. "You've been here before?"

He nodded. "A few times, but trust me, this is my favorite visit of them all."

She stared at him in surprise. He was being so sweet. Did he actually like her? She wished she didn't, but she found that so hard to believe. He reached out his hand toward her. What was he doing? Was she supposed to take his hand? Or did he want her to pass the salt? She panicked. He kept reaching. He had really long arms. She put her hand on the table, in close proximity to his, in case that was in fact what he was after. He took her fingers in his and she thought her heart might stop. He opened his mouth to say something, but a server interrupted.

Hannah ripped her eyes away from his to look at the man standing beside her table. She thanked him for the water that he put in front of her plate, but then when he asked if they would like to try the house wine, Hannah panicked. She didn't know how to respond. When had she become such a bumbling idiot?

"Would you like some wine?" Logan was staring at her.

"I don't think so," she said, her words clipped.

"Okay then." He smiled at the server. "No wine yet, but I'll take a coke." He looked at Hannah. "Coke?"

"Just water's fine." She hurriedly took a sip as if to prove she was really excited about sticking with the water. The server left and Hannah put the water glass down on the white table cloth. She decided she might as well come clean. "I'm sorry, I don't know why I'm so nervous. Part of it is this place, I think." She looked around the gorgeous room and then her eyes landed on him. "Or maybe it's you."

His eyes twinkled. "I'm flattered that I can make you nervous. I could've sworn, a month ago, you hated me."

"A month ago, I didn't know you." She realized she was staring at his lips.

He gently squeezed her fingers. "If it's any consolation, you make me nervous too."

Her heart leapt. She didn't know what to say to that.

"I've been trying to think of a way to tell you, Hannah Carter, that I like you. You intimidate the heck out of me, but I like you. I think I've liked you for quite some time. I just didn't realize it." His voice got softer. "I think I might even more than like you."

A deep peace settled over her, like a soft blanket that she could feel on the inside. The feeling started in her eyes and traveled all the way to her toes. She felt so comforted, so warm, so safe, like she was right where she was always supposed to be. She'd come to Nashville to become a successful songwriter, to have the career of a lifetime, but maybe there was a higher power at work here, and maybe that higher power had brought her to Nashville so that she could be here right now with this man. "I think I might even more than like you too." Her voice sounded like a new version of itself, a rawly honest, throaty version.

He laughed, his eyes sparkling. "Look at us, a couple of wordslinging songsmiths. People pay good money to hear how we make words dance, but we just sounded like a couple of seventh graders."

She smiled, only a little insulted. "I feel a little like a seventh grader right now."

He nodded. "I guess I do too, but seventh grade isn't so bad." He stared into her eyes. "At least, the scenery's good."

Her cheeks got hot.

He sat up straighter. "You know, I was going to write you a song, but I stopped myself."

"Oh yeah?" She narrowed her eyes, waiting for a punchline.

"Yeah. Remember that time I went on and on about how I just fill my songs with utter rubbish that I think will sell? How I'm never actually honest?" He waited for her to catch up.

It didn't take her long. "I do remember. You thought that if you wrote me a song, I wouldn't believe it."

He raised an eyebrow. "Would you have?"

She thought about it. "I don't know. I guess that, if you told me that something was true, I would believe that it was. But you're right, if you didn't preface it with a promise of authenticity, I might have doubts."

He didn't say anything for a long time, and she started to feel self-conscious. Just when she was about to blurt something, anything, out to interrupt the silence, he said, "If we're going to be spending more time together, I should warn you that there will probably be shenanigans. But I can also promise you that I will always be authentic with you. You make me want to be real, Hannah Carter."

Chapter 42

It was the perfect evening. Logan wasn't too proud to admit how happy a good steak made him, and no one made a better steak than Stephen's Steakhouse. If he didn't think about how much it was costing him, it was a slice of heaven on earth, a buttery, juicy steak that practically melted in his mouth. And that wasn't even considering the lobster tail, asparagus spears, and creamy white wine sauce on top of the steak. He hadn't even gotten to those treasures yet. There was also something suspiciously good about the mashed potatoes. What could they possibly put in potatoes to make them that good? He took a drink of his coke and stared at his beautiful date. He couldn't believe how different she looked with her hair down.

She seemed to be greatly enjoying her less pricey truffle mac and cheese. He hoped she hadn't felt obligated to order something less expensive. He was fairly certain he would pay any price to see her happy. She was finally loosening up, acting less nervous, and more like herself, alternately insulting and praising all the songs currently on the charts. He'd heard most of these opinions before, but he didn't mind hearing them again. And as she talked, he found himself more motivated than ever to write a song that would impress her.

She eventually came to Branch Bronson's current hit, which she lauded loudly enough for nearby tables to hear. He was glad she was praising Branch instead of criticizing. He didn't want to offend any of their fellow diners, and one couldn't swing a short stick in Nashville without hitting a Branch Bronson fan. "That man can sure turn a phrase. I'm glad he wants to record one of your songs, but I'm also surprised. I wonder if he's just getting too busy to write now that he has his own record label and everything."

Logan tried not to be insulted and almost managed. "Yes, I would guess that's the case. That's probably why he's trying to write on the road."

She looked up from her handmade penne pasta. "How do you know that?"

Oops. He thought about dodging the question, but he'd promised honesty only minutes ago. He set his fork down. "I know that because Branch asked me to go out on the road with him. To write."

Her chewing slowed and she seemed to have trouble swallowing. "What?"

"It's no big deal. I said no. I can't leave Otis."

She let out a long breath, obviously relieved. "Oh."

"But if I'm completely honest, I didn't want to leave you either."

She didn't try to hide her surprise.

He held up a hand. "Sorry, I'm not trying to freak you out. Here's the whole story. He actually said I could bring Otis, but I can't, because of his treatments, and I'm certainly not going to go without him. But yeah, when I heard the invitation, I was honored, but I didn't even hesitate to turn it down. Even if Otis wasn't in the picture"—he shuddered at the thought—"I wouldn't want to leave you for that long."

She was less talkative after that, and he worried that he'd pushed too hard too fast. Maybe she wasn't as serious about this as he was. He would take things slow, get it right. They finished eating, speaking only occasionally about how good the food was, and soon their server appeared to ask if they wanted dessert. Hannah tried to protest, but Logan talked her into it. He wanted the cheesecake, and he didn't want to eat alone. Nor did he want to share his cheesecake. The server gave them a few minutes with the dessert menu, and eventually Hannah settled on the Ooey Gooey Chocolate Lava Cake. They had a good laugh at how goofy that name was, and then they waited in a fairly uncomfortable silence for their sugar to appear.

When it did, they dove in, and took turns moaning about how good it all was. She made such a good case for the lava cake that he ended up needing to try it, which led to him sharing his cheesecake after all, and it turned out he didn't even mind. He couldn't believe he'd found a woman he was willing to share his cheesecake with.

Chapter 43

Hannah's knuckles were white on the steering wheel. She was trying to predict the future, and she was failing. If he had picked her up, then he would have dropped her off, walked her to her door, and then kissed her. She knew this. But that's not the way this had happened. She had picked him up. And now she needed to drop him off. So, did she, as the woman, offer to walk him to his door? That would be super lame, wouldn't it? But if she didn't do it, then maybe he would think she didn't want him to kiss her. And she *really* wanted him to kiss her. She couldn't wait for that. She was also scared to death of it. What if she did a bad job of kissing him back? She hadn't kissed anyone in ages.

She considered taking the long way home—give herself more time to think about it.

"Wow, you do know that there are police officers in Nashville, right?"

She looked down at her speedometer and took her foot off the pedal. "Oh, whoops." She'd been simultaneously thinking about taking a long detour and speeding to get to that kiss. What a loon.

He snickered. "Are you in a hurry to get home?"

"I don't think so." She didn't know what to say.

She pulled into his driveway still undecided. Her eyes landed on his truck. "Would you like some help washing the paint off your truck?"

He made no move to get out of her car. "What, do you mean right now?"

Her face got hot. She didn't know. Was that what she'd meant? She was struck dumb.

"May I kiss you?"

She'd been expecting a kiss. She hadn't been expecting him to ask permission—permission that she desperately wanted to grant, but her mouth wouldn't cooperate.

"It's okay if the answer is no. Obviously, I want to have a relationship with you, but I'm also happy to take this slow."

"No," she blurted out. She'd meant *no*, she didn't want him to get out of the car without kissing her, but that's not how it had sounded, and that's not how he had taken it. "I mean yes!"

He laughed.

"Sorry, I meant that no, we don't have to take things slow. I mean, we can take things slow but not so slow that you don't kiss me tonight." She leaned her head back on the headrest and closed her eyes. "Oh my word, why am I so bad at—"

Before she could finish the question, his lips were on hers, and they were the best lips in the history of all lips. They were soft, warm, gentle, and they tasted like sweet cheesecake. She turned her face toward him and rested her hand against his cheek, which was pleasantly stubbly from his five o'clock shadow. She tilted her head and pressed into the kiss. He slid his arm behind her back and pulled her into him as he massaged his lips with hers. It was the perfect kiss. She couldn't believe she was kissing Logan Hawkins, and she never wanted to stop.

He pulled away, smiling. "That was awesome. I think we should have tried that a long time ago."

"Maybe." She realized she was breathing heavily and tried to get a grip.

He put his hand on his door and leaned away from her. "Good night, Hannah. Talk to you tomorrow."

"Wait!"

He stopped, expectantly.

She reached out and grabbed the front of his shirt. "Kiss me again. I think we can do better."

He grinned. "You're such a perfectionist." Then he leaned in and kissed her some more.

Epilogue

L oretta (Lettie) Washburne had been flattered when she and Cole had been invited to Branch Bronson's bar-b-que. But then they *arrived* to Branch's bar-b-que and realized that he'd invited all of Nashville.

Branch had rented out Jake's Bar-B-Que Joint for his latest album's launch party, and Lettie was excited to feast on Jake's specialty: baby ribs. They would be messy, but they would be worth it. She found a table near a wall and settled in, but her husband quickly scooped her up. "Let's go outside." He grabbed her hand and pulled.

"It's so hot out!" She didn't protest too much, though, and soon they were outside in the bright sunlight, heading across Jake's backyard.

"I want you to meet the people who wrote 'Can't Lose You,'" Cole said.

Oh cool. She really liked that song. He stopped in front of a man and a woman who each had a dog on a leash. She liked them immediately. People who brought their dogs to album launch parties were her kind of people. She held out her hand. "Hi, I'm Lettie, Cole's wife."

The man took her hand. "Hi. Logan Hawkins, and this is my girlfriend and songwriting partner, Hannah Carter."

Hannah shook her hand too. "It's a pleasure to meet you. I'm a big fan of Cole's."

"So am I." Lettie smiled.

One of the dogs jumped up and planted his paws on Lettie's thighs.

"Otis!" Logan cried and yanked him back down. "Down!" Looking disgusted, he shortened the lead. "So sorry about that."

"He's got some spunk," Lettie said.

"You have no idea. And only months ago he was battling cancer." Looking like a proud papa, Logan reached down to pat the dog's head. "But now he's fit as a fiddle."

Lettie looked at the other dog, a hound who looked bored with the whole affair. "And she's a little less spunky?"

Hannah grinned broadly. "Indeed. But she's perfect."

"I believe it."

"Nice to see you both," Cole said. Then he looked at Lettie. "Come on, there's someone else I want you to meet." He dragged her away from the cool couple, and she was sad. She wasn't much for small talk, but they'd had dogs. She promised herself she would drift back toward them if she got the chance.

She shook hands with the two men Cole wanted her to meet next, but they were total snoozes, so she found her mind drifting away from the conversation. Logan and Hannah took their dogs to the fence, away from the crowd, probably in case they needed to do their business, and this brought them closer to Lettie's ears. She didn't intend to eavesdrop, but she couldn't help it. They were so sweet together.

Logan kissed Hannah and said, "I think I like you, Hannah Carter."

"I think I like you too."

He kissed her again. "I think I more than like you."

She giggled like a school girl.

"In fact," Logan said, "I think I love you."

"I think I love you too," Hannah replied and then pressed her lips against his.

The dog named Otis barked, as if giving his stamp of approval, and Lettie thought, *What a perfect little family the four of them make.*

More Books by Penelope Spark

Sweet Country Music Romance
The Rising Star's Fake Girlfriend (Lettie Jameson's story)
The Diva's Bodyguard (Maggie Hammer's story)

Clean Billionaire Romance
The Billionaire's Cure
The Billionaire's Secret Shoes
The Billionaire's Blizzard (Branch Bronson's story)
The Billionaire's Chauffeuress
The Billionaire's Christmas

Penelope also writes as Robin Merrill:
Shelter Trilogy
Shelter
Daniel
Revival

Piercehaven Trilogy
Piercehaven
Windmills

THE SONGWRITER'S RIVAL

Trespass

Gertrude, Gumshoe Cozy Mystery Series
Introducing Gertrude, Gumshoe
Gertrude, Gumshoe: Murder at Goodwill
Gertrude, Gumshoe and the VardSale Villain
Gertrude, Gumshoe: Slam Is Murder
Gertrude, Gumshoe: Gunslinger City
Gertrude, Gumshoe and the Clearwater Curse

Wing and a Prayer Mysteries
The Whistle Blower
The Showstopper
The Pinch Runner

www.ingramcontent.com/pod-product-compliance
Lightning Source LLC
Chambersburg PA
CBHW022126170626
46808CB00002B/861

* 9 7 8 1 3 9 3 6 9 9 0 4 0 *